LIONHEART

LIONHEART

Thorvald Steen

Translated by James Anderson

LONDON NEW YORK CALCUTTA

Seagull Books, 2012

First published as *Løvehjerte* by Thorvald Steen
© Forlaget Oktober, 2010

English Translation © James Anderson, 2012

This translation has been published with the financial support of NORLA

ISBN-13   978 0 8574 2 033 6

British Library Cataloguing-in-Publication Data
A catalogue record for this book is available from the British Library

Typeset in Arno Pro by Seagull Books, Calcutta, India
Printed and bound by Hyam Enterprises, Calcutta, India

CONTENTS

Thanks to Athir, Behaeddin, Bosporus University, Jean Floris, Halldis H., Kari V., Arne R., Steven Runciman and to the descendants of Saladin and Richard I.

King Richard I lay in a four-poster bed, above him the dark blue velvet canopy was embroidered in gold with stars and a half moon. He was in the small French castle of Châlus-Chabrol. The wound in his left shoulder had turned gangrenous. He had received the injury during a minor skirmish in front of the castle gates. Richard was forty-one years old and hadn't a single grey hair.

His closest aide, Hubert Walter, who a few days later was to become chancellor, thought that the king 'looked as if he didn't understand the gravity' of his situation. The king's mother, Queen Eleanor of Aquitaine, stood at the bedside. In her hand, a stick mounted in silver. Her face powder was unevenly applied and some of it fell from her cheek. She had clearly put it on herself, having recently been displeased with her ladies-in-waiting. Richard saw a tear driving the make-up down the folds of her chin. The old woman brushed her thin fingers over the powder. Richard asked to be left alone. They didn't listen to him.

Some are comforted by the thought that other people can see their sufferings. Richard wasn't one of them. He couldn't sleep. His voice barely audible, he told the doctors to refer to the herbals and textbooks on pharmacy by the nun Hildegard of Bingen. They didn't know her work. They were considering amputation but couldn't decide. The risk that he might bleed to death was considerable.

Richard told them to fetch a priest. He wished to confess and receive extreme unction.

Outside the open window, behind his mother's back, the green leaves moved almost imperceptibly. The sun was already high in the sky on that warm spring day of 1199. His gaze rested on the shadows the leaves threw on the wall. A breeze transported the vaguely sweet scent of lavender to him.

'I hear that you weren't wearing armour,' his mother said.

Richard stared at the wall. She stroked his cheek. He turned his face away. She bent over him glancing sideways to make certain no one else could hear.

'You will get better, Richard. You are the world's greatest Crusader, you are the conqueror of Jerusalem.'

'I have something to confess,' he said.

'Rest now.'

He closed his eyes. Suddenly he felt cold. It was simply a harbinger of the final, great desert, he thought. The practiced, repeated, whispered. It almost felt like a relief.

I
JERUSALEM

They rode through the long shadows as the sun went down. The mountains about them shivered. For a while he could see their outline, until they burnt out and darkness reigned. They made camp. Close by, an emaciated dog yelped. Its hind legs were broken. A horse had trampled it during a battle. It dragged itself forwards like a seal. The dog whimpered all night.

When the mountains took shape far off, he made up his mind. He found the brown and white dog behind a bush. With his face averted from the trusting eyes, he killed it with a club. The sole witness, a snipe, stood flicking its tail.

The sky was naked and blue above them. Grey clouds came from nowhere, three bolts of ball lightning swept sulphurously past. Not a single raindrop fell. There was enough sand to bury the dead.

1

Richard and his mother Eleanor had been visiting in Brest. She suggested a ride to the coast. It was overcast, a chilly wind blew across the Bay of Biscay. From his saddle he kept looking down at the high pigskin boots his father, King Henry II, had given him for his eleventh birthday, he'd sent them from London. Richard was extremely proud of them. The grey breakers had crests of foam. They passed several long, white beaches and came to a low cliff. There were just the two of them, the great sky and the sea.

His mother reined in her horse. Richard did the same. She told him to undress. He folded his clothes, placed them neatly in a pile and peered down at his pale, freckled body. Eleanor told him not to be frightened, she would teach him everything. Before he could reply she'd thrown him in. The icy water paralyzed him. He didn't float, he swallowed water, he floundered, his arms and legs went numb, he sank, it turned black, he was sucked down as if in a funnel, slowly, soon his arms ceased flailing, there was a pressing at his ears.

When he came to his senses, his mother was standing over him in dripping wet clothes, crying. She said she'd leapt into the waves, dived, swum down and, just as she'd been about to give up, his right arm had floated up, as if miraculously, towards her, she'd got hold of the small boy-ish hand and swum to the surface and the light, hauling his slender body after her.

'You're alive, it's God's will, Richard. God gave me strength. He made your hand reach out to me. God wants both of us to be his servants. Do you want to be God's servant, Richard?'

'Yes, Mother.'

'Of course you do.'

She kissed him, stroked his hair and kissed him again and said that she loved him.

'God doesn't want me to learn to swim,' Richard said starting to cry.

She kissed his fingers.

Suddenly he felt his mother gripping his arms. He was thrown in again. It wasn't long before he was shouting:

'Mother, I can swim!'

'Thank God,' said his mother and brushed the hair from her forehead.

Her look was distant.

He wasn't at all sure she was aware of him.

'You are God's chosen one and will perform the tasks he sets you once you are King of England.'

He repeated his mother's words to himself.

'Now we must dry ourselves.'

She pulled a blue woollen blanket from the horse's saddlebag. His teeth chattered and he was shivering. She dried his hair and rubbed him all over with the blanket. He turned away, glancing down at his small, protruding member and fixed his gaze on the boggy landscape that surrounded them. His mother hummed the lullaby she'd sung to him every evening during his early years. His throat was sore and he felt dizzy. She rubbed him harder and embraced him once more. How good she smelt, was it roses? His mother told him to get dressed. She turned away, pulled off her clothes and quickly dried herself. Richard stared at her pale back. She had freckles on her shoulders just like him. He had never seen her naked before, he caught a glimpse of her hips before she wrapped the blanket round her body and faced him. He turned quickly towards the waves, and said something about the sea which he couldn't even remember himself. She picked up the shawl she'd thrown to the ground and wrapped it round her hair.

'We must get indoors before we take cold.'

The sun broke through the layer of cloud and warmed them. She placed her wet clothes in the saddlebag and, wearing only the blanket and the shawl, rode ahead of him. Richard had never seen a woman who could ride better than his mother. She rode like a man. They found a barn where they could dry her clothes. While the wind and sun did their job, his mother sat clasping him on a bench below the barn. She stroked his hair and back. He pressed more tightly to her. His mother said she was proud of him, and that one day he'd be King of England and the entire Angevin Kingdom.

He stared into his mother's green eyes, before noticing that her long, curly red hair had dried.

'But surely, Mother, Prince Henry is to be the next king, he's older than me.'

'God will take a hand. Neither King Henry nor your brothers have a faith that is fully committed to the Crusades. That was why I didn't want to live with your father any more, and why you and I left London and came to Poitou. God has decided that he won't live all that much longer.'

'But what will God do to Prince Henry?'

'Allow him to die. God wants the best endowed among you to lead the Crusade against the Saracens. Ever since you were born, God has seen that you are fit to fulfil his wish. The archbishop of Canterbury and the pope's envoy agree with me. My first husband, King Louis VII of France, little Prince Philip Augustus' father . . .'

Richard thought he knew what his mother was talking about.

'Is he the one who likes to be called Philip?'

'Yes, but don't interrupt. Philip's father tried to be a Crusader. He was hopeless. I was in the Holy Land with him and I saw it with my own eyes.'

'Did you have armour, Mother?'

'A suit of the very best. Let me finish. Your father has always opposed the Crusaders. Did you know that he was responsible for the murder of the late archbishop of Canterbury, Thomas à Becket?'

Richard looked at her horrified and shook his head.

'How do you know that my brother is going to die?'

'Our Lord told me in a dream. How it will happen is his secret.'

She embraced him and fixed him with that determined expression he knew so well. He was in no doubt.

He would be England's next king. No matter what Prince Henry and his father might do.

'Promise me that as well as practicing with your sword and bow, you'll always read and write poetry. Even the strongest man isn't much good if he knows nothing about feelings, in love as well as in gauging where his enemy's weakest point lies.'

She fetched her clothes and dressed behind the barn. Richard thought she was beautiful. The way she looked him in the eyes, nearly always made him do what she wanted.

'Mother, you won't ever desert me, will you?'

She gave a start. She came towards him with resolute steps, placed her hands on his shoulders, looked straight at him and said:

'Never.'

2

As soon as the umbilical cord was cut on 8 September 1157, there were three things his parents were in agreement about: the infant was a well-grown boy, his hair was red and his name would be Richard. They repeated the name as they displayed him to the cheering crowds at Winchester, Canterbury, Nottingham, York and London. They disagreed about everything else.

Eleanor was thirty-five when she gave birth to Richard, his father twenty-four. By her first husband, Eleanor had had daughters Marie and Alix. In 1152, she divorced Louis VII and eight weeks later married Count Henry of Anjou. Richard's father was heir to the English throne after King Stephen of Blois. Henry had inherited the Countships of Maine and Anjou and the Dukedom of Normandy. Eleanor ruled Aquitaine, comprising the Countships of Gascony, Guyenne and Poitou. With England as well, this became one of the three most powerful kingdoms north of the Alps.

The two rivals were France, consisting of Flanders, Champagne, Blois and Burgundy, with Paris as its main seat—and the yet more powerful Holy Roman Empire of Frederik I Barbarossa. The Holy Roman Empire bordered France and Champagne in the west and Russia in the east.

South of the Alps the dominant power was the Byzantine Empire where Emperor Manuel I was undisputed ruler.

Eleanor gave birth to five sons and three daughters, Matilda, Eleanor and Joan, between 1152 and 1167.

When Eleanor asked her husband one last time to support the Crusades and was given no for an answer, she moved out of Winchester Palace, taking Richard with her.

Richard believed that his parents never annulled their marriage because each felt certain of outliving the other and inheriting everything. It wasn't easy being a child, Richard was fond of saying, when your mother and father were at the head of warring armies—even if the dining hall was a large one.

At the age of twelve Richard was betrothed to Princess Alys of France, Prince Philip's elder sister. The engagement was concluded after talks between Eleanor and her former husband. The engagement was sanctioned by King Henry, who invited Alys to come and live in London.

All their lives the brothers quarrelled about inheritance, titles, lands, goods and castles. Princes Henry and John were their father's favourites. He could never come to terms with Richard and Geoffrey. William had died at the age of two. The one thing Richard and his brothers could agree on was that a compromise is an agreement in which you pretend to give way. A war avoids this.

The only one of his siblings Richard liked was his half-sister, Marie de Champagne. She was twelve years his senior, blonde and with green eyes and not quite as tall as her mother. She was keen that her half-brother should get as much education as possible. When she said he ought to read Ovid, Socrates, Plato and Aristotle, he took it as an order. Marie had confessed to him that Marie de France was her own pseudonym and that she'd written the books *Les lais*, *Fables* and *L'Éspurgatoire de saint Patrice* about courtly love. Marie impressed on him that to win a woman's heart a man had to be heroic, chivalrous and noble.

Although Marie meant much to Richard, no one was more important to him than his mother. Eleanor had convinced Richard that he was a recruit on the side of good against evil and that he had only one overlord. His mission was to be ready when God summoned him to arms against his father and the Saracens.

3

Five years later Richard stood and studied his mother's hair, which fell across her slender shoulders. With the light behind her he could see the reddish tinge of her curls. Eleanor was wearing a blue woollen cloak. It had a collar of fox skin. She halted her horse before him. Her back was so straight. He raised his arms to help her down.

'Do you remember the first time I took you on my lap and told you about the Crusaders, and about the knights in armour who could turn their lances against the Saracens?'

'Jump! We can't stay out here too long. My father's men are only a quarter of a day's march away. You don't want to be discovered before you cross to the French coast tonight.'

This was the second time Richard and his mother had met after King Henry had imprisoned her for 'conspiring against the Crown and serving the interests of a foreign power'. After pressure from the Church she'd had her imprisonment commuted to house arrest on both occasions. Both times she absconded to meet her son.

'Do you like Alys?' Eleanor asked.

He nodded as he thought of her brother, Philip. Richard and Alys had gone to Paris to meet her father.

Richard had liked King Louis VII because he'd said nice things about Eleanor. He'd said that they'd separated because she hadn't borne him sons. But after they'd married again, they'd done very well, said the king, laughing and looking at Philip and him. Richard was envious of the younger prince's self-assurance, he who was so certain of being the future monarch of France. It was Philip and not Alys he'd spent most time with in Paris. They'd been good days.

'Alys is beautiful, isn't she?'

'Yes,' Richard answered.

'Would you consider marrying her?'

'In a few years' time.'

'Your father's sleeping with her.'

Richard lowered his arms.

He felt his face and neck turning red. It was his mother who'd been keenest on the engagement. His father supported it because there was a lot of political advantage in good relations with France. He hoped this would allow him to gain control of Louis and his kingdom. The fact that his father had no moral scruples was nothing new. But Richard found it irritating that he'd even begun to think about his father again.

Richard felt a pain in his forehead. He recalled so vividly the first time he'd had a headache. He'd been five years old. His father was in company with several friends, earls and counts who were indulging Richard. They said that they wanted to play with him and show him something he'd find really exciting. Right at the top of Winchester Palace was an open window. Richard was all unsuspecting.

Suddenly, his father lifted him up and held him at arms' length out of the window. Richard wailed. His father and the other men laughed.

The memory filled Richard with nausea.

'I'll put an end to your father's antics,' said his mother. She looked straight at him. 'You've got a father you don't deserve. From now on, God will be your only father.'

'Yes,' Richard answered as his mother jumped.

He caught her with outstretched arms and set her down safely on the green turf. They held one another for a long time, looked into each other's faces, smiled, embraced again and laughed.

'I've written my first poem.'

Richard positioned himself in front of his mother, his arms behind his back. He had to say it from memory. What if she didn't like it? The worst thing would be if she started to laugh. But perhaps it would be almost more painful if she smiled, the way adults did when children were acting grown-up. Richard realized that he was more frightened than if he'd encountered an experienced knight in battle. He drew breath.

'I asked a boy with a candle: "Where does that flame come from?" He blew it out. "Tell me where it went, then I'll tell you where it came from," he said, and left the room.'

Richard just managed to glimpse a shadow before he received a blow to his temple. When he came round, he was lying on the ground with his arms tied behind him. His face felt swollen. He just managed to raise his head before three men pushed it down again. His mother was held fast by several soldiers.

'Do you know who I am?'

'Yes, indeed we do, Ma'am,' said the officer who was holding the standard with its three lions. 'You and your son are under arrest for treason. We've been following you for the past few days, ever since you broke your house arrest.'

The officer kicked Richard.

At first the soldiers had hesitated to lay hands on Eleanor, but when she began lashing out to help Richard, they got her to the ground and tried to gag her. She continued to fight even after she'd been hit in the face several times. The officer drew his sword and placed the point on her throat.

'You're the lackey of a king who will soon be dead. God will punish both him and you,' Eleanor screamed.

They carried her struggling to a closed coach which had been drawn up. As soon as she'd been manhandled in, the door was locked.

Richard's arms and legs were manacled. He yelled. His invocations against the king got no further than the tightly stuffed wad of cloth in his mouth. They carried him down to a cellar. Three days later he was taken across to Barfleur on the Normandy coast and set free. His mother ended up in an unknown prison in England.

His father could not have hurt him more. Richard would never forget her fury as they forced her into the wagon. What he remembered most of all, though, was the despair in her voice when she realized that perhaps they'd never see each other again. She sounded resigned. He'd never heard her like that before. His father had taken the only person Richard really loved. If his father executed her, Richard would burn London and put him to death in front of his other children and the entire court at Winchester. But if his father didn't kill her, what would he do then? It didn't take Richard long to realize that his father had to die before his mother could be free. Prince Henry wouldn't be allowed to inherit the Crown after the death of his father. Never. His elder brother would be allowed to abdicate in favour of Richard, or die. He was doing God's work. Unlike his father or brother! Now at last he was grown up. From now on he had to finish the task alone. His mother, the pope and God were waiting for him.

His mother wasn't executed. In June 1183, Prince Henry got dysentery and died a few days later. That same evening Richard went on his knees and begged God's forgiveness for not trusting his mother fully and completely, when she'd said that Henry would die. Then he asked God when the king would die but he received no answer. Geoffrey breathed his last after a tournament three years later. When he died, King Henry wrote to John:

My dear son,

It is my greatest regret that you are not older than Richard.

4

The head and body lay enveloped in blood and fluid inside a bulging, dark sack. The nose appeared first, then the forehead, neck, back, belly and finally the shuddering, weak legs. The helpless newborn lamb was licked clean by its mother. As soon as the membrane had gone the lamb tried to stand. It fell.

Richard had never seen a lamb being born. He stood in full armour next to three pages he was training with the lance. With purposeful strides he went across to the newly born lamb and tried to raise it up. The ewe butted him. Bewildered, he toppled backwards on to ground.

The apprentice knights got him to his feet. The groom helped him off with his equipment, while Richard stared at the creature that so much wanted to stand. After some faltering, it managed to get to its feet. After staggering for a few steps it began to walk. Richard followed the lamb out of the stable. A thin column of smoke rose over the flat fields of Anjou. The smoke came from a pile of burning leaves a little way off. Richard heard voices, he turned his head and saw three unknown men standing just behind the groom.

One was Jacques Breton, who represented the poor of the countship. The other two were a bishop and a carpenter.

'Good Richard, Count of Poitou and true heir to the throne of England, we have great trust in you. We know you hate injustice. We have come here to . . . Well, we're risking a lot by speaking to you. You hold our lives in your hands . . .'

'Speak out, Bishop.'

'Your father is a man who does not always keep his word.'

'Has that ever happened?' Richard interrupted, as his eyes followed the lamb's tottering progress back to the stable.

A stone's throw away, the River Loire glided quietly past.

'I'm not sure just how I ought to put this,' said the bishop. 'But on this side of the Channel too, we, the men of the Church, think the king is someone who . . .'

'. . . Tells lies,' put in Jacques Breton. 'Don't mince words.'

'King Henry has burdened us with new taxes, unreasonable taxes. You are the man of the faithful and of the people. We hope you will raise an army.'

'Why does he treat you like this?'

'He wishes to give the nobles the right to flay us and then take his share from them.'

'Do you want me to go against my father?' Richard asked.

The young pages, the groom and the three men glanced furtively at one another. Richard smiled.

'So the bishop believes one needn't always obey one's father?' Richard said.

The bishop ran his hand over his stole.

'Our Lord is above even our parents,' he said earnestly.

'Friends, I jest,' said Richard laughing.

The men facing him began to laugh, cautiously at first, and then with greater conviction. Richard could hardly have received an inquiry that suited him better. If the Church and the common man begged for his help, it wouldn't only be noticed in Anjou but throughout the whole of his father's realm. He would conquer with God's help, anyway. At last the battle against the Saracens' allies was about to begin, and foremost among them was his father.

'How many men and weapons can you lay hold of?' Richard asked.

'Thirty pages, a few knights and somewhat fewer squires and grooms. But we'll be able to assemble a good many men on foot. And we've got three crossbows in first-class condition, with the finest iron bolts.'

'That's not a lot, Bishop. You realize that if we fail, we'll all lose our lives?'

Richard's voice was clear.

'Certainly,' said Jacques Breton before the bishop got a chance to reply.

'But how many men does my father have?'

'Far more, at least three times as many as us,' said the carpenter.

'We'll get more than a thousand foot soldiers,' Breton added.

'But have you got weapons for them all?' Richard asked.

He noticed that Breton hesitated.

'No,' said Breton at last, dropping his gaze.

'There are two things in our favour,' Richard said. 'If we act quickly, the king will have great difficulty in gathering all his forces. In addition, our army will have the most to fight for.'

'You too?' Breton asked, surprised, and turned his eyes on Richard.

'I don't simply want to prevent my father from robbing you. I intend to kill him. He won't obey God's command to take part in the battles in the Holy Land.'

The men stared at him in astonishment. Richard broke the silence:

'Are we agreed that we'll draw up our troops early tomorrow morning, just after sunrise?'

Everyone nodded.

The three men had overestimated how many would take part in the campaign. The whole army numbered three hundred and twelve souls, including women, children and older men, according to Richard's count in Chinon marketplace the evening before the battle.

Richard stood on a bench. As he opened his mouth, it was if the Holy Ghost entered it and filled him with limitless strength.

'Tomorrow we attack the enemy forces. They are camped just outside Tours. Tonight we begin our march.

Those you will defeat do not fight for the Cross in the Holy Land. They fight to enrich themselves, whilst you, good citizens of Anjou, pay the very greediest of them with your toil. Even though the force you will meet is that of the King of England and Count of Anjou, know that God rules over him and that God is on our side.'

The bishop nodded and made the sign of the cross.

That night the small army lay down to sleep a quarter of a day's march from Tours. Richard woke a little after midnight and looked at the full moon before turning on his side. There was a knot of tension in his chest. His breath came quicker. Was he afraid? Could they lose? The whole of his poor army lay about him on the ground, in their undergarments. Was this what they would look like dead, ready to go to purgatory? He slapped his cheek. Of course they'd win.

The enemy was waiting outside the walls of Tours. Richard was insistent that everyone should be dressed as soldiers, whether they were squires, grooms or knights. Several mules and horses carried riders made of straw and wood, under helmets, capes and mail. His father's men were drawn up on open ground. His army was at least three times as large. King Henry II was nowhere to be seen.

Richard gave orders that they were to march and ride side by side so as to give the impression of being more numerous than they were. He shouted 'stop' when they were within bowshot of the enemy. Here they were to remain and await further orders.

Richard passed the word for Jacques Breton and asked him to bring his sister, Sara. Both were dressed in clothes that belonged to Richard. Sara Breton had tied her long, brown hair into a knot beneath her helmet. As protection against arrows and sword thrusts she wore a padded jerkin she'd borrowed from one of Richard's pages. She was strong after years of labouring in the fields. Richard asked her to ride by his side. She was a skilled horsewoman. He told the brother and sister that they were to ride with him to the front line where he would make the enemy an offer. If it failed, they would have to ride back to their own forces as quickly as possible.

Richard told Sara and Jacques that they had to display an exaggerated self-assurance to dent the enemy's fighting spirit. Furthermore, Richard knew that he possessed two advantages that his father's commander didn't have— he wasn't afraid of being outnumbered. In fact, he positively relished it. The second and decisive asset was that he had his own motivation to win. Even if the army he was to meet was only a small portion of his father's total strength, it would be a humiliating defeat for the king. If Henry fell in the battle, and the mere thought of it caused a smile to break across Richard's flushed face, he would proclaim himself king.

Richard rode one horse's length in front of Sara and Jacques towards the enemy's ranks. Jacques carried Richard's and the Count of Poitou's blue-and-white standard. When they were three horses' lengths from King Henry's army, Richard raised his hand. Jacques and Sara halted. Richard rode forward to the enemy commander.

'I notice my father isn't here. I have the bishop with me,' Richard said pointing. 'That shows which of us has God on his side.'

'You're bluffing,' said the commander, an elderly, grey-haired man.

Jacques Breton heard what was passing. He turned and shouted to the bishop:

'Show them your cross!'

The bishop took out the silver cross he wore on a chain round his neck. He held it aloft. The cross shone. Richard noted that several of the men glanced uneasily at their commander.

'Show us the bishop!'

The commander cleared his throat. The knight at his side removed his helmet and mopped the sweat from his brow.

'They don't believe people like us can have the bishop's support, they'll never believe us,' Richard heard someone behind him shout.

It was Sara Breton's voice. A stone flew through the air and struck the bare-headed knight in the face. His horse reared, the knight was bleeding from a cut on his forehead. He gained control of his horse and rode at Sara. Half his face and one eye was covered in blood. Enraged, he wielded his sword. Richard went after him. Just as the man was about to strike, Richard's sword severed his thumb. The man screamed. His sword fell out of his hand. Richard placed the point of his sword on the man's throat.

'Go! See what happens to those who defy God. This time it was your thumb, next time it will be your head.'

The man disappeared at a wild gallop. Richard rode back to the commander.

'We've been lucky with the weather,' he said.

The commander was silent.

'What's it like serving a master who opposes the church and is such a coward that he keeps his devout wife prisoner for three years? I have a suggestion. Send a carrier pigeon to my father. Tell him that you met a superior force and that you would have been wiped out if you hadn't stopped in time.'

'To battle! Charge!' shouted the commander.

Richard rode at him and drove his sword into the man's side, where he wasn't protected by mail. The man fell off his horse and lay motionless on the ground.

'Be off while you still can, and tell your tax-collector that I've rescinded his decree,' Richard shouted.

The commander's lieutenant turned and yelled:

'Retreat!'

The soldiers nearby looked at him questioningly at first, before fleeing with the rest of the well-equipped army.

The victory meant more to Richard than anyone could know—no matter how hopeless the position, he could win. He realized that this was no great military triumph, but he was sure that it would enhance his reputation as a fearless and idealistic fighter.

That same afternoon Richard rode at the head of his force to one of his father's castles near Tours. Ten soldiers had been left to run the castle and its domains while King Henry II was in England. Richard chased them off and let his army feast on the food and wine within. They prepared pheasant, carp, bread and sweetmeats from the stock in the castle's larders. Jacques maintained that it wouldn't feed them all. Most of them had gone hungry over the past few weeks, he explained. He asked Richard to help him get hold of a few sheep. At first Richard didn't know what he was talking about. Jacques disappeared momentarily and returned carrying a knife and a hammer. About twenty sheep were grazing in the meadow. Jacques ran to the nearest one and got it in a stranglehold. It bleated and kicked. Jacques squeezed tighter.

'Take the hammer and bash it on the head.'

Richard hesitated.

'Now!'

He got it first time. The sheep closed its eyes. Jacques slit its throat. This was repeated until four of them had been slaughtered.

The sheep were flayed and butchered. The largest joints were roasted on spits outside the castle. The offal, some of the meat and the heads were boiled in four large pots in the kitchens, and placed on dishes. The sheep's ears lay like withered leaves on their cheeks, mouths gaped, light-red tongues stuck to the teeth in their lower jaws, the teeth were only just visible between the twisted lips. The cuts of meat and the offal were like garlands round their heads and were bathed in fat. Half the army had gathered around Richard and Jacques.

'Keep away, the food's not ready yet!' Jacques shouted.

Richard and Jacques were shoved aside. Even though Richard ordered them to stop, they bolted the whole lot. Only then did Richard realize how little he understood his soldiers.

That evening Sara Breton asked how Richard could know that he had God on his side. Her brother tried to hush her up.

'When God saw our "army", he must have smiled and thought it was a strange procession which deserved to win,' said Richard just as a large quadruped came bounding into the hall where they were eating. Several of the company cried out in alarm and ran. After a while the creature reached the guests of honour and placed its white paws on the table between Richard and Jacques. Richard saw the light blue eyes and the long muzzle.

The creature put its paws on his shoulders and licked all round his face with its pink pennant of a tongue.

'What's this?'

'A dog, mainly, mixed with a good bit of wolf. But it's sweet-tempered and brave. I've used it to hunt my landlord,' Jacques said.

Its head and body were covered in curly, grey hair.

'It's only a puppy,' he added.

Richard rose from the table and went out to get some fresh air. The animal ran after, and past, Richard. Its movements were loose-jointed and immature, as if it wasn't sure where its feet would land when it ran. Its eyes were small and partially covered by hair. It seemed that with every bound it was rejoicing in its strength and balance, Richard mused.

Jacques ran after them between the tables and through the door. He found Richard on his back on the turf.

'That's enough, Wolf!'

'Don't take him away,' Richard called.

Jacques stood watching.

'I've seen wolves,' said Richard. 'They snarl. This dog understands its lineage but is trying to behave. It's strange, isn't it—lots of people should have more wolf in them when they meet sheep in men's clothing. You know what I mean?'

Jacques looked wonderingly at Richard and said:

'Wolf is yours if you want him.'

'Thanks,' said Richard.

Roused by his victory at Tours, Richard gathered a bigger and far more experienced army to overpower his father and usurp his authority in Normandy. The aim was to force him to set Richard's mother free. But his father had skilful scouts. Rather than punish his son, he wished to regain Richard's trust. His father appointed Richard commander of his army. Richard accepted the offer. The French army moved into Aquitaine. Richard's forces defeated them and took the fortress of Taillebourg which almost everyone believed was impregnable. This brought him a renown that came to the notice of the pope.

5

Richard studied Chrétien de Troyes, who had just been reading aloud from his new work. It was a grey, chilly day in Anjou. It was 9 November 1187. Marie de Champagne was holding a literary salon at her mother's palace where Richard lived with his mother's court while Eleanor was in prison. Richard was standing with Marie and her husband, Philip of Alsace, Count of Flanders, as well as Chrétien de Troyes, who was fussy about his clothes, from what Richard could make out. Marie introduced Chrétien to Richard.

'What, Sire, do you think of contemporary English poets?'

'I don't speak English,' Richard said, noticing that he sounded unnecessarily brusque.

'You are sole heir to the English throne and your mother and half-sister have told me that you are also a lover of poetry.'

'I haven't read any of them,' said Richard quietly.

'That's nothing to worry about,' Chrétien said. 'It's a hopeless language for writing good literature.'

The poet had long, well-combed black hair, his eyes were brown, the cloak he was wearing was of fine, crimson wool. Round his neck he wore a black silk neckerchief. A gold brooch on his cloak bore Marie and Philip's monogram. They were his patrons.

Chrétien de Troyes was the court's foremost poet. Author of *King Arthur and the Knights of the Round Table*, *Lancelot* and the love story of Érec and Enide.

Marie wanted to talk about the courageous knight, Yvain.

'Don't speak of that, let us speak of your brother instead,' said the poet nodding at Richard. 'I admire your bravery. Your skill in the field must be famous on both sides of the Channel and in the rest of Europe.'

Richard shrugged his shoulders and tried to smile. Perhaps he wasn't afraid to wield a lance or a sword, but the courage to read two, or perhaps three, of his own poems to the famous writer—that he didn't possess. The conversation turned to the origins of troubadour verse. When they spoke of Bernard de Ventadorn, he could keep up but when Ibn Hazm and the Caliphate of Córdoba were mentioned, he was lost. He folded his arms on his chest. To leave would be uncivil. He didn't want to hurt them, especially not Marie.

Chrétien, Marie and her husband spoke of the twenty small kingdoms in al-Andalus where Christians, Muslims and Jews lived side by side. Richard didn't know what they were talking about. Surely, they couldn't mean that good, Christian believers could live with Saracens? Chrétien, in particular, went even further. As Richard understood him, it seemed that Christians and the others drew mutual benefit from one another. He was about to ask if that was what he really meant. He changed his mind. He must have misunderstood. There must have been something he'd missed. He kept quiet. Even the Moors, Muslims though they were, had given poetry, music and song a prominent place at these courts, according to Chrétien. And each had a well-paid court poet.

'Could that be something for you, Chrétien?' asked Marie.

Christian and Muslim writers cooperated, Chrétien explained, and Ovid was the great literary ideal.

Richard shook his head and pretended it was all old hat. He heard a horse and looked out. A man jumped from the saddle right at the bottom of the castle steps. Richard and the other guests ran out. The man, whom Richard had never seen, was breathing hard, then he crossed himself and said:

'I am Pope Gregory VIII's envoy. My name is Cardinal Lefevre.'

Another rider came galloping into the yard.

'I have terrible news,' said the cardinal. 'After crushing our army at the battle of Hattin in July, Satan himself has taken Jerusalem.'

Marie clasped her heart.

The tall cardinal related that thousands of Christian brothers lay dead on the shores of Lake Tiberias. They hadn't stood a chance. The enemy's horses and soldiers had been too quick. The armour that encased the knights had become a lethally cumbersome carapace. Count Renaud de Châtillon and Guy de Lusignan, whom the Crusaders themselves had made king of Jerusalem, were led into the tent of the Muslim sultan, Saladin. Saladin had drawn his sabre from its diamond-encrusted scabbard and driven the blade into Renaud's breast. This had been pure revenge, according to the cardinal. Saladin sent Guy back to Jerusalem. While Count Raymond of Tripoli, who had made several peace agreements with the sultan, was allowed to flee.

'What a traitor,' Richard said loudly.

Richard noticed that he was standing on tiptoe while the cardinal spoke. He felt himself getting hot. Richard felt no fear; limitless strength invested his head and body. The moment he'd been waiting for ever since his mother had taught him to swim and he'd learnt he was the chosen one, had arrived. God should know that he was more prepared than any human being before him.

With resignation in his voice the cardinal continued:

'The Saracens took Jerusalem without a fight, thousands of Christians and Jews joined the enemy ranks quite voluntarily. And not only that. Listen to this—the sultan invited everyone, regardless of faith, to pray to his god in the Holy City. He promised that all holy places would be allowed to stand untouched.'

The latter arrival turned out to be an abbot. Richard didn't catch his name. The man was powerfully built, but at least a head shorter than the cardinal.

'Your Eminence, I have long known this moment would come,' Richard cried.

The cardinal and the abbot gave him a questioning look. The abbot's face was white. His thin hair looked like smoke as it stuck out from the side of his round head. The cardinal began reading the French translation of Pope Gregory VIII's bull:

"'Wherefore, sinners, listen carefully to my words. The ways of the Lord are unsearchable. Saladin has taken us by surprise. He has advanced against our king, our bishops, our Knights Templar and Hospitaller, barons, inhabitants and the Holy Cross. Take Jerusalem. Bring the Cross back to where it belongs. Surge forward.'"

Quietly, Richard whispered to the abbot: 'What was the sultan's name?'

"'The next Crusade must begin immediately, or the Devil will rule the world. The Holy City must be reserved for Christians once again. The more Saracens you kill, the shorter your journey to Paradise. The highest place in Paradise will be reserved for the man who brings Saladin's head to Rome and lays it at my feet.'"

'That will be me,' said Richard.

God was leading him, he didn't need his mother by his side, this was between him and God, all power was concentrated in his head and tongue.

Marie looked at him.

'Mother would be proud of you now.'

Richard was pleased at what she'd said. He turned to the cardinal.

'Tell Pope Gregory that I myself will lead the army as soon as I'm King of England. I will sell castles, privileges, towns, yes, even London itself to raise money for the Crusade. Tomorrow I shall take the Cross in Tours Cathedral.'

'But isn't your father still living?' the cardinal asked.

Richard smiled at the sight of the bewildered face.

'Your Eminence, you, in your dealings with the pope and his master, ought to know that my father's days will soon be numbered. Tell the pope that I shan't beg a heretic king, who holds captive the devout Queen of England and Duchess of Aquitaine, for anything whatsoever. Say that I expect the pope to get my mother released and to ask my father to abdicate.'

6

In May 1188, Richard and King Philip of France made a pact for 'eternal friendship and military cooperation'. Richard attacked his father's forces in Poitou. King Henry replied by attacking King Philip's territory.

Philip was twenty-four, eight years younger than Richard. He had already been king of France for eight and a half years. Philip was short compared to Richard, and his hair was dark. His left eye was blind. Philip was no great fighter. But he was good at employing able military and civil leaders. He was far more sociable than Richard.

On 3 June, they joined forces and marched towards King Henry's army. The pope was against this war. He thought that England and France would do better to join forces in a Crusade. The war lasted two months. It led to little except the deaths of fourteen thousand soldiers and many more civilians. During a short-lived peace the border was moved a few hundred yards, in a landscape that for most of the year was cloaked in mist and rain. Two months later the war flared up again. Queen Eleanor managed to smuggle a letter out to her son on 11 June. Richard found it on the chair in front of his writing table, unable to account for its arrival.

Dear Richard,

Your hatred for your father is quite understandable and laudable. But why stoop to his level? Augustus wrote: 'Life is a pail of shit which only gets fuller, and one we must lug along with us until our final moment.' If you succeed in taking Jerusalem, all will be yours. It is God's war against the Devil that Frenchmen and Englishmen want to take part in.

Richard read the letter several times. In the beginning, he was uneasy. It was the first time they had disagreed. There was no question that it was her handwriting. Did she fear losing some of her privileges when he'd killed his father?

So it seemed he was capable of making decisions that went against his mother's interests.

He smiled at the thought.

Dear Mother,

So good to have a letter from you, I miss you. Mother, you taught me to be honest, even with you. I must take my revenge. It will give me extra strength before I set out for the Holy Land. Many of Father's soldiers will come over to me.

His quill came to a sudden stop. All at once he realized that he didn't know where to send his reply.

Barely a day's march from Chinon, where King Henry's army was camped, Richard and Philip stood watching the smith who was repairing their lances. It was as much as the sun could do to penetrate the mist and open a pale eye, before closing it again. Richard heard three horses approaching. He turned away from the anvil. Philip and Richard caught sight of a grey and white skew-bald and its rider. Richard could tell from a long way off that the man on horseback didn't enjoy riding. But what a beautiful animal he was mounted on, with its big, strong body propelling its head proudly into the wind, nostrils flaring and ears erect, its large eyes looking straight ahead.

The man was followed by two soldiers riding a horse's length behind him. They held two white pennants high above them, as well as King Henry's standard. As they drew nearer, they could see that the rider leant uncomfortably and unnaturally forwards. He was an elderly man. Philip had never seen him before. Richard recognized him as soon as he had, with some difficulty, dismounted. The sun shone through his horse's sweeping tail. The man bowed and came a step closer. It was the Earl of Essex. Richard felt as if a black cowl had been pulled down over his head. Would his father attempt peace negotiations? I won't agree to that for all the world, Richard thought.

'Sire, I represent His Majesty King Henry of England, and . . .'

'Say what you've come for!'

'The king wishes to meet his son.'

'I'm not disposed to negotiate either a truce or a peace!' said Richard.

'The king wishes to talk to you about everything except this war.'

'We've got nothing to lose by you talking to him,' Philip whispered. 'We need more money for our joint crusading army. A bit of tractability on your part may surprise you father's allies and cause a rift among them.'

'Do you remember when you, your father and I played bowls outside Windsor Castle?' the Earl asked. 'Of course you've learnt much from Queen Eleanor and her daughters, but it was your father who played with you, more than anyone else, during the first few years of your life. No one has played more horse-and-rider than you two. Do you remember when you got your first lance, a small one, of course, from your father?'

Richard felt anger and disgust at the way the old man chose to descend to the level of sentimental moments from his childhood.

'We're at war,' Richard answered.

'He was patient with you, your humour wasn't all that . . . Ah, well, he took you with him into the forest and told you about the animals. Have you forgotten that it was he who taught you to read?'

'Does he want to ask pardon for what he's done to my mother? For supporting the Saracens? For dangling me out of the window?'

'He wants to talk father to son.'

'Get out.'

The Earl told his two henchmen to help him on to his horse.

On 5 July, Richard and Philip's forces managed to take the fortress at Tours. The next day, while they were standing outside the weapons' tent, a messenger arrived from King

Henry II's court at Chinon. The messenger related how the king had clutched his breast and told the monk who was sitting by his bedside, to write: 'I hate the day I was born, and all my sons. None of them has ever listened to my counsel. I also hate this day, long and grey at both ends.' Then he died.

Richard closed his eyes before raising his arms above his head and shouting:

'Thank you, Lord, for being with me.'

The messenger asked if there were any message to take back to the court at Chinon.

'Say that I am England's new king and that the coronation will be on the third of September. My mother shall sit by my side. She is to be freed immediately and liberally compensated.'

Richard tried to pronounce the words as calmly as he could, so as to hide his ecstasy. Philip mustn't see that the title of king meant so much to him. He began pacing up and down with his hands behind his back, looking now at the ground, now up at Philip.

'Have you thought about what you're going to do about the Jews, Richard? Your father got a lot of help from them, as far as I'm aware. What will you do with their leader . . . what's his name?'

'Jacob of Orléans. He says he won't supply money for the Crusades. I will refuse all Jews access to my coronation.'

Richard stopped, raised his head and continued:

'Now that I'm King of England as well, Philip, is there anyone more powerful? Now the Crusade can begin. We'll set out within three months. You agree?'

Richard didn't wait for an answer.

Philip glanced at a thrush that was taking off, and said:

'The alliance between our houses, Richard, must be the strongest there has ever been in Europe. You must be our leader when we make war on the Saracens. You are the experienced soldier.'

Richard appreciated Philip's subservience. In a way it was natural, age and ability considered. But he couldn't deny that this acknowledgement of his own power and leadership within the alliance further enhanced his self-confidence. Although Philip was charming and possibly meant what he said, he was naturally also a player in the game for mastery of Europe. All apparent intimacy, even temporary subservience, was nothing other than a means to achieve something more, something much greater, of strategic significance, for his own family and for the country he ruled. Philip needn't pretend otherwise. He mustn't imagine that Richard was stupid. Philip might be young, and his family might have enjoyed many untroubled years on their throne, but there were limits.

'Do you remember when we sailed across the Seine the first time we met in Paris?' Philip laughed. 'You'll have to do something about your seasickness before we leave, Richard.'

'I rid myself of that a long time ago,' Richard lied. 'And you, Philip, you'll have to learn how to swim.'

7

Richard seated himself on the throne directly in front of the sacristy, with his face turned towards the rows of pews in the cathedral. The light slanted in through the high, oblong windows. He got up and seated himself again. He'd done it a bit too quickly the first time. It was such a glorious feeling. Could he do it one more time without it seeming odd? Could Philip see him? No, he appeared to be sitting talking to his queen, Isabel. One doesn't question what a king may do. He did it again. The only reason he regretted his father's passing was that old King Henry should have been sitting at the very back of the cathedral watching his son triumphant on the dais, with all his old vassals present, and worrying if the new king would acknowledge them. Had any Jews managed to sneak in? He didn't know what they looked like.

The great doors were thrown open. There was the sound of a fanfare. He felt a hammering in his head and chest. It was the king's mother arriving. Richard was sure that nobody was more impressed by his mother than he was. Was she more like a bride or a queen as she approached him step by step? He threw a quick glance at the people applauding on both sides of the aisle. How many of them had advised the old king to have her executed? His mother knelt before him. He rose, took her hand, told her to stand and gave her a long embrace before leading her to the throne that stood next to his own. Fifteen years of incarceration hadn't visibly altered her appearance. At sixty-seven, this woman was still upright and red-haired. She'd got a few more wrinkles around her eyes but that was the only change. Did seeing her son as England's king make her radiant? Behind him choirboys sang while the public found their places. Richard recognized few of the guests. He glanced at his mother, she'd been crowned Queen of England on the same throne she was sitting on now.

Eleanor smiled at most of the people who walked up the central aisle and bowed, first to Richard, then to her, before being shown to their places by a chamberlain. Certain people she didn't nod to. He tried, first in a whisper, and then louder, to ask why she didn't want to greet everyone. The choir drowned out his question. His mother motioned to a guard and whispered something in his ear. Shortly after, five of the guests were escorted out of the cathedral.

'Some Jews managed to get in,' whispered his mother.

The cathedral was decorated with epergnes of blue gladioli. Large, three-branched silver candlesticks along the walls were lighted as darkness crept in. All the royalty and nobility of the British Isles were present.

When everyone was seated, the archbishop of Canterbury, Baldwin of Exeter, emerged from a room behind the sacristy. He made the sign of the cross, and greeted first Eleanor and then Richard. Then he turned towards the public and began speaking. It was English with a bit of Latin thrown in. Richard hardly understood a word.

He glanced at Philip who was whispering something to Isabel. They obviously understood nothing of what was being said either. Richard was irritated with himself for not giving orders that people should use French and Latin.

Richard had wanted a grand coronation. 'Ensure that it will make the guests forget my father,' was the injunction he'd given Hubert Walter, who was then a bishop. Walter wasn't just a learned theologian but also a lawyer. He was nephew to King Henry II's Justiciar, the country's top minister, Ranulf de Glanville. Walter had been his uncle's ablest clerk. At the same meeting, Richard had asked the bishop if he would accompany him on the Crusade. Walter promptly answered yes, and said that from now on Richard wasn't just England's king. He would also usher in a new era of achievement that would outshine that of his father. The coronation would form 'the very portal of Richard's time as uncontested king of the Crusades'.

Richard smelt burning as he strode solemnly out of Westminster Abbey, spectators cheering on both sides. He asked Eleanor if she knew where it was coming from. She shook her head. Philip stood at the door and bowed.

Outside, Richard could see that there were fires in several parts of the city. One of the guards said that several Jews' houses had been set alight by his own soldiers. Rumours had been circulating that the new king wished to punish Jews because they wanted nothing to do with the Crusade.

Just as the king's cortège was riding along by the Thames, a man was chased out into the icy water. Richard was told that he was a Jew. The people waiting for the king

to pass, ran down to the bank. The cortège was forced
to halt.

'Help! I can't swim.'

The majority just stood there cheering. A few
shouted:

'You lot crucified Jesus!'

The bald man in the waves had gone under twice
when he shouted:

'Down with King Richard!'

'What's he saying?' Richard enquired of his adjutant.

One of the king's household troops raced up, threw
himself into the water, hauled the man ashore and gave
him a beating. Two soldiers took charge of him. The wet
trooper ran up to Richard and said something he didn't
understand. Richard nodded. It was taken as a death sentence for high treason. One of the guards asked if there
was a priest in the crowd. Several came forward. The one
selected asked the bald man if he would convert and
receive extreme unction before his execution.

'Why?' demanded the man.

'God wishes it,' said the priest.

'How do you know? I'm the one who'll soon be
talking to God.'

Next day Richard learnt from Hubert Walter that the
learned Jacob of Orléans had been beaten to death.
Richard shrugged his shoulders. Only when the massacre
had degenerated into chaos did Richard deploy his guards
to bring calm to the streets of London, before the farewell
dinner for King Philip and Queen Isabel. They were to

travel to Paris the following day. It would look bad to the guests if he hadn't got control of his capital.

The two kings ate for a long time before they began to talk.

'I didn't realize that you were so frightened of the Jews, Richard?'

'I think they're the ones who are frightened of me.'

Philip assumed a distracted expression before mumbling:

'If Noah had been able to see into the future, he'd have sunk the ark, don't you think?'

Richard was about to ask what he meant.

'How far have you got with preparations for the Crusade? Remember that the pope has asked us to return with the Cross. We two are the ones in whom he has confidence. What do we require for success?'

'Ignorance and self-confidence,' Philip replied.

After Philip and Isabel had left the gathering, Richard watched Hubert, who was talking to his mother. They seemed to get on well together. He was pleased about that. Richard went over to them.

'Take care that Philip doesn't try to wriggle out of the Crusade. Don't underestimate his cunning, my son,' Eleanor said. 'We must make sure that he doesn't take our territory while you're in the Holy Land.'

'I'm not worried,' said Hubert Walter. 'Philip knows that the aristocracy will rise against him if he doesn't go.

The pope will excommunicate him and denounce everyone who trades with his subjects. Once you have taken Jerusalem and killed Saladin, Richard, Philip's nobles will beg for your protection and leadership as well. France will be ours.'

Richard agreed. He nodded and told Hubert Walter to find out if the soldiers and constables had quelled the disturbances outside. Walter bowed and left.

'Do you know, Mother, some of my returning knights say that Saladin is incapable of hatred.'

Eleanor considered, clasping her hands and wringing them until they gave a small crack.

'I don't believe it. In any case, hate is requisite for a ruler. But it must be pure.'

'My hate shall be purer than his.'

'It's never been a problem for you so far, Richard. But watch out. Hate is a powerful emotion, just like love. It can cause confusion in our minds.'

'What makes me uneasy, is that more and more believers say that there's something special about him. They respect him.'

'Don't let a war get personal. That's one thing you ought to have learnt from your father. He never let anything get personal, not even when he fathered four sons.'

She had never been sentimental. Without a laugh, without so much as a smile to accompany her words, the sentences fell.

'Promise me you'll take the knights who are the most experienced soldiers, not those who just want to put on smart uniforms.'

'As far as military matters are concerned, I'd rather you didn't involve yourself, Mother.'

'It won't happen again.'

'But what if I lose?'

'You're not serious?'

Richard could tell from her face that this really was an unthinkable notion for her. But was she right? Where he hesitated, she was merciless.

'An arrow could find me in an unlucky moment.'

'It won't happen. God will protect you, my son.'

'But he might be thinking about other souls at that moment.'

'He will always watch over you. But you know that perfectly well, Richard! Didn't you sleep properly last night?'

Richard recalled how certain she'd been that his father and Prince Henry would die to make way for him.

'With your faith, breeding, fervour and skill with the sword and lance, you will return the greatest of all heroes. You've got it in you to convince the doubters and return home as the foremost prince in Christendom.'

Richard nodded.

'To mollify John's greed and jealousy I've decided to grant him lands in Derbyshire, Somerset, Dorset, Devon, Cornwall and Montaine in Normandy and to make him Earl of Gloucester.'

'Wise king,' said his mother.

8

Richard was swimming with a couple of bodyguards near Caen, when they were hailed by a man on the shore. He was waving his arms and calling for the king to come immediately. It was midsummer. At last the weather was hot. The man had come from the court of King Philip. He had two things to communicate. The first made Richard laugh with joy.

Like Richard, the Holy Roman emperor, Frederik I Barbarossa, had immediately obeyed the pope's exhortation to join the Crusade. With more than a hundred thousand men he marched south from Regensburg. It was a well-rested army with the finest weapons and good supplies of food along the route. It caused the brothel industry in Swabia, Bulgaria, Trakya, Constantinople and all through Anatolia to flourish again.

Everything went to plan. The army was well organized and they all obeyed the emperor as their unquestioned leader. On 10 June 1190, the great, red-bearded, sixty-eight-year-old emperor was about to cross River Saleph at its shallowest point. The weather was fine, the temperature pleasant and there were no tricky currents in the water. It was simply a matter of wading across. A few yards from the bank the emperor dropped down dead. Whether it was his heart or some other problem, his soldiers didn't know. In growing desperation they attempted to revive him, but to no avail.

The sight of the dead emperor caused half his forces to flee. Those who continued the march to Jerusalem found it hard to part with their old leader. It was therefore decided that he should be placed in a coffin full of vinegar. The vinegar would preserve the corpse. The bier accompanied the onward march. The emperor was carried high all the way, over mountains, down valleys, across wild, torrential rivers, in all weathers, to the principality of Antioch, which was controlled by the Crusaders.

Prince Bohemond received the remnants of the army as it came marching up the dusty main street. The emperor came first, borne by ten men. Ranged around the deceased were twenty men on horseback, with Frederik I Barbarossa's flag. Behind the emperor's remains marched his son with bowed head. The stink from the coffin reached all the way up to the Prince's stand.

When the emperor's flesh fell off his bones, the archbishop of Antioch persuaded his son to bury him, allowing that five of his father's bones should accompany the onward march to Jerusalem.

'There you see!' Richard said when the envoy had related these events. 'God wants me, and not Frederik, to save Jerusalem.'

'The other thing I was to deliver from the pope was this,' said the envoy, and handed Richard a container with a parchment inside it.

My noble Queen Isabel died quite unexpectedly on 9 March 1191. Her soul went immediately to Paradise. Our departure must therefore be postponed, Most Royal Majesty.

Richard read Philip's words aloud several times, then swore and cursed the fact that Philip had once again tried to delay departure. The envoy asked if there was a parchment to take back. Richard merely asked him to say that the message had been received.

That evening Richard picked up his quill and wrote to his mother:

Philip is like my father, a man who is a believer only when it suits him. Now he's exploiting his queen's death. Deep down Philip has always hated this Crusade. It sickens me that I must take him with me. Pray for me. You will be proud of me, Mother, I promise. It won't be long before the world can say: 'Richard I, the king who won Jerusalem back for the pious.'

The big difference between Philip and me is that I look forward to going into battle for God. I know that I shall win. These are my feelings, but not his. Every evening before I sleep, I pray for you, Mother, and for our Lord. And after I've prayed, I imagine you and our Lord cheering as I ride into Jerusalem. For three years, ever since the pope asked me to free Jerusalem, I've had this dream. While I wait for Philip, I'm exercising my knights and soldiers in close combat.

If only his mother knew how restrained the letter was compared to his agitated thoughts. She must believe he'd managed to become calmer with the years. Eleanor and Bishop Walter had insisted that Philip and his army take part in the Crusade so that he wouldn't pose any threat to Richard's kingdom on either side of the Channel. Philip had even helped to make the decision, but no one had foreseen what would happen afterwards. Hundreds, perhaps thousands, of believers were dying weekly in battles with Saladin's forces in the Holy Land, whereas the pope's allies hadn't even set out. The whole world must think that he and Philip were cowards or in the service of the Saracens. Philip was a coward, certainly, but not he. Why shouldn't he simply go to the Holy Land alone without Philip's men? He could defeat Saladin and return home before Philip could mobilize an army and attempt to conquer England. And, after he'd dealt with Saladin, he would have the whole of Europe on his side and Philip would be crushed for good. What a parade and entry he would have when he rode into Paris with his entire army!

After mulling the matter over, Richard decided to give Philip one last chance and sent a messenger to him with a clear ultimatum. If he didn't turn out immediately, Richard's forces and all the other countries that supported him would be ready to invade France.

One evening in Bayeux, Richard heard that the troubadour Bertran de Born was singing scurrilous ditties about his and King Philip's tardiness—'The Tortoises with the Cross' was the title of one. Richard's seasickness was another theme. Philip wasn't lampooned as frequently in these songs. Richard assumed this was because he hadn't been so vociferous in his support of the good cause. He decided to visit the tavern where de Born performed.

The place was dark. Neither de Born nor anyone else recognized Richard. After the entertainment he went over to the landlord and said that if de Born wasn't barred from singing there from now on, the tavern would be burnt down. The owner acquiesced at once.

Philip received Richard's message and recognized its sincerity.

9

In the summer of 1190 they set out, with an army of just over seven thousand men. The kings agreed to divide the lands they conquered. Richard recalled the next few weeks as pleasant and productive. Philip and he talked about the time they'd both been princes and had lived an almost carefree life, and about how different they were, that yet they liked one another, and how vital it was that they put disagreements about the date of departure behind them. They must appear inseparable. They embraced, they would be friends for all eternity. Richard couldn't remember Philip being more charming and sprightly. He had even begun to tell stories about Normandy, a place they both loved and had visited innumerable times. They spoke of the Norwegian, Rollo, a Viking chieftain who in 911 became the first Duke of Normandy. Rollo, forefather of William the Conqueror, was given Normandy by the Carolingian monarch Charles the Simple. Richard and Philip laughed at the nickname.

Richard's sister Joan joined the royal entourage for the sea voyage from Reggio di Calabria to Sicily's largest port, Messina. Joan and Tancred had been betrothed by their respective fathers some years previously. The idea was that Richard would hand over the dowry as soon as he landed at Messina.

Tancred welcomed them with over-elaborate compliments, thought Richard. After a short stay in Messina they all continued to Palermo on horseback. Joan asked to speak to Richard alone on several occasions. He asked her to wait. He wanted to negotiate various things with Tancred at once. Tancred insisted they should wait until the banquet the next evening at Palermo. As host, he claimed he had that unwritten prerogative. Philip persuaded Richard to play along with it.

Tancred had only one eye and a decidedly crooked nose. He was small and hunchbacked and almost bald. And, as if his appearance wasn't enough, he was aggressive, stubborn and grasping.

With his first toast in Palermo, Richard reminded Tancred about the nuptial agreement. Tancred opened his arms wide and said that the agreement was invalid because it had been worked out by their deceased fathers and not by themselves. The world had moved on. Richard said that Tancred's refusal was an insult to his sister, nodding at Joan. She turned scarlet. Richard wasn't sure whether from anger or relief. Tancred's arrogance angered him more than a little. What was he thinking of, this man who wasn't striking a single blow for the Crusade? And whose only interest was profiting as much as possible from the Crusaders who had to anchor in Messina for supplies on their way to the Holy Land? Tancred replied by demanding a dowry twice as large as the one originally agreed. Richard hurled his wine in Tancred's face and left the hall. He took Joan with him.

Richard thought that Tancred ought to be punished for breaking his pledge. The fact that Tancred wasn't willing to supply knights, soldiers or financial help to Richard and Philip's Crusade, didn't ease his temper. That evening he decided to take Messina. Philip refused to take part. He tried to calm Richard by telling him that they needed supporters now, not more enemies.

'You haven't changed,' Richard said sullenly.

Richard led the charge against Messina himself, with his own army. The city fell after three days. Tancred was forced to pay twenty thousand pieces of gold and another twenty thousand for a wedding between one of his daughters and Richard's nephew and heir, Arthur, Duke of Brittany. The marriage was to be a recompense for his broken engagement to Joan.

A fortnight later King Tancred organized a reconciliation banquet. Philip and Richard sat next to each other. Joan didn't wish to attend. Tancred made several attempts to talk to and toast Richard. But he ignored the Sicilian king. Hors d'oeuvre of fish and octopus, which he'd never seen before, were served. The main course was more familiar, consisting of wild boar and venison.

Assortments of fruit were brought in. There were many fruits, whose shapes and colours were quite new to him. Their beauty and fantastic, almost comical, shapes, their skins that were thick or thin, with or without prickles and patterns, held his entire attention. A rosy yellow fruit with a soft, downy skin was cut in half. He was taken aback to see the large, grooved stone inside it. The flesh was juicy with a fine, slightly sour, taste and smell. After eating the fruit he sat weighing the stone in his hand. What a gift God has given mankind in his work of creation, he thought. Such fruits didn't deserve to be eaten. They were too beautiful to be stuffed into the mouth, chewed to a pulp and gulped down the throat, into the stomach's darkness. Richard looked for someone who could tell him the names of the fruits.

Philip bent towards him:

'Isn't it about time you married my sister Alys? You've been engaged for almost twenty-one years now and, well, she's not getting any younger.'

'I'm tired of this fuss about marriage.'

'Fuss? It's been several years since it was last mentioned.'

Richard stood up suddenly, went outdoors and tried to vomit. He stood there looking out across the waves. It was grey and drizzling. But no foam crests. A bird came flying in from the sea. It was a heron. It was coming towards him. He noticed how it flew with its head and neck hunched in between its shoulders. It's just like Philip, he thought.

The days came and went, with storms and rain that prevented them from setting sail. Richard was in despair about the delay. For his part, Philip was more concerned about what they were having for dinner.

One evening, without warning, and to Richard's great astonishment, Eleanor arrived. She and her party had managed to sail at night when the sea was calmer, from

Reggio di Calabria to Syracuse. Mother and son met at a castle on high ground behind the town, with a view of Malta. The queen of Aquitaine appeared, from what Richard could discern, to be in fine fettle despite her lengthy sea journey. Richard was genuinely pleased to see her. He caressed her cheek a good many times before they embraced. A couple of paces behind his mother stood an unknown woman and a cluster of servants. She observed Richard with a watchful gaze. She had black hair and large, brown eyes. He assumed she was a lady-in-waiting.

'Who's she?' Richard asked, nodding towards the strange lady.

'You seem interested.'

'We haven't got a lot of time, Mother. I'm leading a Crusade.'

'Isn't she lovely?'

'Is it possible to know what she's called?'

'Berengaria, the king of Navarre's eldest daughter. She's going to be your wife.'

'Now?'

'Yes. It's advantageous for both Navarre and England.'

Richard decided that Philip and his fleet should cross the Mediterranean directly to the Holy Land. Richard's fleet went via Crete, Rhodes and finally Cyprus. The wedding took place in Limassol on 12 May 1191. Richard and Berengaria exchanged vows, before the bishop of Evreux crowned her Queen of England. Immediately after the ceremony Eleanor sailed home.

When the wedding celebrations were over and Richard and Berengaria were alone at last, Richard told her that he and the army would have to weigh anchor next morning. The pope, all the nobility of Europe—knights, barons, counts, princes, dukes—they were all waiting for him. Berengaria stared at her husband in wonder.

'There's a night before the dawn, my king,' said the Queen of England.

Once the door to the bedchamber had been shut, servants and household soldiers fell to their knees before the keyhole. They prayed that the newly-weds, with God's guiding hand to help them, would provide England with a well-formed prince.

Richard had never seen a naked woman, or man, whose skin was so dark. Her hair was curly, her eyes large and expectant. His gaze flickered over her until it settled on the tapestry on the wall behind her. Now the Saracens would be massacred and their lives filled with force and meaning. The thought of the decisive battle he would wage against the Saracens in Jerusalem caused a bubbling within him. Richard picked up a large, yellow silk shawl his mother had given Berengaria just before the wedding and draped it round her body.

'I'm going out for a walk,' Richard said.

It was dark outside. He walked down to the harbour, just beyond the castle. The ships were ready to sail the next day. As quietly as he could, he climbed over the rail of the nearest vessel and stood right on the point of the bow. He wanted to try to accustom himself to being on board before the long crossing. Out at sea it would be far worse.

There was hardly any wind. It might have been blowing a good deal harder, he told himself. He shouldn't worry about it.

The waves caught his attention. They weren't big. At least, not those he could make out by the light of the half-hidden moon. The night sea was black, it rocked, not much, but a little, undulated, as if covering itself with itself, floating plates of iron that collided silently, blending into one another. Not long since, he thought, the rays of the evening sun had been reflecting bronze on this water that wasn't blue but bottle green, before turning darker and darker, until it was now black and impossible to distinguish from the deck. He looked up. He could make out the contours of the mast as it lazily pointed to and fro at the starry sky, from one constellation to another. His stomach heaved. He vomited. He held on to the rail, spat and decided to go ashore. His feet had no sooner touched the quayside than he was overpowered by three soldiers. Their torches illuminated his face.

'Aren't you . . .?' one of them said. 'Sire, didn't you get married today?'

'You've seen nothing. Do you understand?'

10

The first sentence read: 'His full name is Salah al-Din Yusufubn Ayyubi.'

Richard repeated the name out loud. Only now, on the final leg of his journey across the Mediterranean, was he able to read about the Antichrist, the man who had to be vanquished. Saladin was the abbreviated form of his name used in this intelligence document from Sir James Sheringham, Sir William Davenport and Count Henry of Toron.

All three were in their third year in the Holy Land. The count had even learnt Arabic. The two English knights spoke and wrote French and had committed the report to paper. Richard knew them of old and judged them to be dependable and well-informed aides.

The weather during the final part of the voyage was excellent, with cloudless skies and a gentle breeze. Today there was a pleasant following wind, and he sat on deck, reading.

Until the age of twenty, Saladin spent most of his time playing polo, studying the Koran and reading poetry. It was his uncle who turned him into a soldier and officer. Saladin was born at Tikrit in 1138.

His parents were Kurds and his father a chieftain. Saladin and his family have never been reconciled to our liberation of Jerusalem in 1099. His uncle, Shirkuh, was a great military strategist. After three strenuous campaigns Shirkuh took Cairo. Saladin served as an officer in the decisive battle. Two months later, during a banquet to celebrate the victory, Shirkuh choked to death on a piece of meat. Caliph al-Adid nominated Saladin as the new vizier because he was the youngest and least experienced of the emirs in the victorious army. The Caliph thought that Saladin would be easy to manipulate. Saladin was given the title 'The Victorious King' and was presented with a white turban shot through with gold thread. In 1169, he became the undisputed ruler of Egypt after defeating a Frankish crusading army south of Cairo. In 1171, he got the Sunni and Shia Muslims to cooperate. Saladin is small and slight of stature, with a smooth, closely cropped beard.

Richard looked a bit further down the page. He followed the words with his forefinger hoping to find a piece of information that he could exploit in the battle with his enemy.

On Friday 2 October 1187, twenty-seventh day of Rajab, 583 after Hejira, on the day Muslims celebrate the Prophet's night journey to Jerusalem—the city the Saracens call al-Quds—Saladin made his entry into the Holy City, supported by a number of Jewish as well as Christian priests. None of our sources, Sire, deny that Saladin actually positioned guards around the Church of the Holy Sepulchre so that it was not desecrated by his own people. In addition, he enjoined the Franks to remain in the city and invited banished Jewish families to return. We cannot tell if he is insane. Al-Aqsa, which had been turned into a church, became a mosque once more after the walls had been sprinkled with rosewater. We know that many of his own people are deeply at odds with his views. We must inform you, Sire, that the pope is mistaken when he states that Saladin can neither read nor write. In our experience he is master of the written word in several languages.

The authors said the following few paragraphs didn't require much of his attention. Richard wondered if they meant that he wouldn't understand them or that they contained trivialities.

Saladin is deeply influenced not only by Islam but also by 'Sufism', the doctrine of the various paths that man can follow to get closer to, and eventually coalesce with, God.

'Sufism,' Richard slowly repeated.

He'd never heard the word before. The aim was self-restraint it said. But surely his mother could have taught him that? Wasn't it reminiscent of knightly virtue?

As he went on reading, his astonishment grew. Asceticism and moderation were its ideals. Jealousy, egoism, pride and greed were reviled. But, he thought, wasn't this something he could have promulgated himself? Further down the report he read:

Saladin's favourite poet was, of all things, a woman. Rabia al-Adawiyya. In 790, she walked through the streets of Basra carrying a torch in one hand and a pitcher of water in the other. When she got home she wrote 'Fire and Water' as a title, then: 'I shall hurl my torch into Heaven, I shall pour my water on the fires of Hell. God must be worshipped in love, never for fear of Hell or the prospect of Paradise.'

Richard read the words several times. She wrote about God as if convinced she was speaking of the one true god. Richard placed his finger on the words that Henry of Toron had translated. It suddenly dawned on him how much he would have liked the text to be his own. He got it off by heart and decided he'd send it to his mother as soon as he was ashore.

Richard took a last look at the report. He admitted that the words had at first perplexed him, then made him uneasy, as if they shone a light on something he hadn't the ability to understand and which was impossible to remedy now. Fortunately, he had God on his side.

11

Richard stood on deck admiring the sand-coloured mountains and hillsides in the distance. He could make out bushes in a few places. That was all. The sun was still high in the sky. The landscape was barren, but he thought it had a special beauty, too. As it approached Acre, the Crusaders' main port, there were two hundred and twelve ships in Richard's fleet. The city lay in the south-eastern Mediterranean, between Haifa and Tyre. The majority of his vessels were cogs with a large, square sail amidships. The captain of his ship warned Richard to be vigilant. They could be fired on by long-range shots from the besieged fortress behind the city walls of Acre.

The houses round the fortress were made of dried clay. For several months Richard's allies, commanded by Count Conrad of Montferrat, had tried to conquer the city and extend the Kingdom of Jerusalem. If Acre could be captured, the faithful would have yet another port through which they could send food and soldiers to and from Europe.

Richard put his foot ashore. He was in full armour, his face almost entirely covered by his helmet. He was sweating. He'd never known such heat. His crown was on his helmet. Three golden lions, one above the other, were embroidered on the red cape he wore over his armour. The pattern was repeated on his shield and on the standard borne right behind him. Richard turned and shouted:

'Follow me, men! The Saracens dare not fire a shot.'

Richard had to shout twice.

He had never felt more motivated. Not a single ache or pain, he noticed, even though he searched carefully. At last they'd arrived. At last his experience and strength could be tested. At last God's meaning for his life would be fulfilled. Nothing was holding him back. Thousands of soldiers and knights stood waiting with raised swords. The Crusaders had been in control of the harbour for several months. But the battle for the fortress was raging. They'd been waiting for their undisputed leader for more than half the year.

Richard's allies rejoiced from the moment his feet touched the sand. He saw all their sweaty, dirty faces. They yelled his name as if he were the Saviour. Just imagine if Jesus had been able to experience such shining eyes, full of hope, Richard thought.

'Men, this is a date we will always remember—the eighth of June, 1191. Within three weeks we'll be in Jerusalem!'

Richard fixed his eyes on Acre's high city wall before turning his face to the commander ashore, Robert de Sablé, Grand Master of the Knights Templar.

'Where are the Saracens?' Richard asked.

De Sablé pointed to the ruins of the city wall, which in several places reached right down to the water's edge where the waves were green and choppy.

Richard hadn't taken many steps on land before he heard the fanfares in his honour. The fever-red glow of the ruined city wall would soon fade. Richard could make out a caravan of camels. The animals were much larger than he'd expected. They had lain down to rest. Their drivers lay next to them in the heat. They seemed unaffected by the temperature.

In battle, Richard thought, when you were being attacked, you could fight back, defend yourself or hide. None of this was any good against the heat. It was everywhere. High, low, south, north, west, east, in the sand, in the rocks, on the roads, in his armour, in his undergarments, skin, throat, neck and head. The report on Saladin said nothing about the heat. A shrew ran across the burning, dry red earth right in front of him and sought shelter in some dry undergrowth.

'What extraordinary clothes,' said Richard pointing towards the caravan.

He'd never seen anything like it. The women wore long dresses, with veils, belts and shawls. The men were wrapped in tunics and capes and had kerchiefs on their heads, held in place by a slender rope.

All afternoon Richard's soldiers and knights leapt ashore from the ships. The gangplanks they'd brought with them were fixed in place and cannons, swords, cannonballs, large amounts of dried meat, salt, tallow and wine were carried ashore. After that they marched to the besiegers' main quarters. Because the crossing from Limassol to Acre had been relatively short, they also brought horses and mules from Cyprus.

That evening there was a feast to celebrate Richard's arrival. The word 'saviour' cropped up in several of the speeches.

Philip came up to Richard and embraced him. King Guy de Lusignan introduced himself as the 'King of Jerusalem' when they met. The others who shared the high table with Richard and Philip, Count Conrad of Montferrat, Duke Leopold of Austria, Count Ludvig of Thüringen and the Duke of Burgundy, didn't feel the need to mention their titles. It was obvious that the others on the tribune were so relieved that Richard had come to their aid that they had no wish to provoke him unnecessarily. The shock of Frederik I Barbarossa's unexpected death made them even more wary. Without Richard and his army, the experienced Crusaders with Robert de Sablé at their head wouldn't have stood a chance.

De Sablé was in charge of the celebration. The English and French standards fluttered at each end of the tribune. The three golden lions of England stood one above the other on a red background. The three French fleurs-de-lis were golden like the lions, although the background was blue. Richard thought it a beautiful sight. He told Philip that he was seldom moved but now he was. The banners of the counts and dukes represented also flapped in the breeze, if less ostentatiously than those of England and France.

'Your fleet looks very fine from here, Sire,' Duke Leopold said in English.

Richard turned to Hubert Walter, standing behind him. Walter translated.

'Merci,' Richard replied.

Berengaria came up to him. They hadn't seen one another since the wedding as they had sailed in different vessels. He asked his queen if she didn't think the ships lying in the harbour were a grand sight. Berengaria replied by asking when she would be able to leave for Anjou which would be her new home from now on, wouldn't it? At least, that was what her mother-in-law had told her.

Her question confronted him with the expectation of many people, especially in England, that the royal couple would live there. He was pleased she hadn't mentioned England. 'Not now,' was all he managed to say before involving himself in a new conversation.

By the end of the evening Richard's entire fleet had anchored up. Now they had to take the fortress and the town.

Sultan Saladin's nephew, Taki ed-Din, was in charge of the defence of Acre. One of his advisers fled and gave himself up to Richard's forces that night. He disclosed the enemy's plans to one of Richard's native servants:

Taki ed-Din had assembled his military council in the ruins of his bedroom. The council chamber had been razed to the ground. After Taki ed-Din had described the gravity of the situation and the tactics his men were to use, he ended with: 'King Richard has terrible force at his disposal, proven courage and an invincible nature. He has never been beaten in previous wars and has gained a great reputation. In the matter of power and prestige he cannot compare with the king of France. But he is richer and braver and has considerably more military experience.

Will this break us?' The question had been answered with a ringing 'No.'

When the defector had finished speaking, he was executed on Richard's orders.

Next morning Richard rode at the city walls of Acre, drew his sword and shouted:

'Attack!'

Richard turned to Philip:

'Hurry. We're almost at our goal. But we're short of time. The pope will be grateful to you, Philip.'

'But do we know enough to attack, Richard?'

'If you're frightened, just keep close to me. The first time you kill, it costs a bit. After a while you don't notice a thing.'

An arrow struck Richard's chain mail and broke.

Burning poles and great iron balls from the Crusaders' army hurtled through the air towards the fortress and city walls. Richard and Philip stood on some high ground and looked over the army. Richard was at first astonished, then disturbed when he saw several knights mounted not on horses but on mules. He asked the nearest officer for an explanation.

'Many of the horses died on the way here. Look over there, Sire,' said the officer, pointing.

At the very rear of the army stood a group of exhausted soldiers who were carrying their armour.

'Their spirit has returned after you arrived.'

'When are they going to put their armour on?' Richard asked.

'When you give the order to storm the walls.'

Richard glanced at Philip. His face was white and sweaty under his helmet.

'Pull yourself together. These Saracens will spread like the plague in our realms if we don't exterminate them. We shall carry Saladin's head back to Rome.'

The Crusaders' army consisted of three sections. Richard kept them all on a firm rein. The first was under the command of the king of Jerusalem. The second comprised Richard's and Philip's forces. The third formed the rearguard and included Duke Leopold's men. In the midst of them were two great siege machines on wheels, which they called 'God's Own Sling' and 'The Neighbour from Hell'. Richard was never told why they'd been given such strange names. Stones were hurled at Acre's walls. The fireballs struck houses, markets, children, breast-feeding mothers, terrified cats, old men waving their arms about and those who were trying to save their lives after the previous night's bombardment.

The Crusaders closest to the city walls fought until they were exhausted. Then they changed places with the section of the army that was furthest away from the walls. These were responsible for obtaining supplies from the ships—loads of weapons and food, like pork, veal, bread, beans, cheese, flour, biscuit, syrup, wine and water. Richard was especially satisfied with the Danish and Frisian men, in addition to his own. These soldiers displayed the best discipline, no matter how badly injured they were.

Infantry marched on both sides of the royal standard which was mounted on a cart. Richard wore a helmet and a crown, as he had when he arrived in the Holy Land, and rode at breakneck speed between the vanguard and the rear, sending out orders in every direction. Richard himself didn't hold back in the skirmishes. This made his soldiers braver.

In a letter written on 7 July, Taki ed-Din begged Saladin, who was waiting on a headland beyond the city walls, for permission to surrender. Richard was demanding two hundred thousand pieces of gold to end the siege, the release of fifteen hundred imprisoned Crusaders and the Cross of Christ. Taki sent the letter by a messenger who swam out to Saladin. For several weeks the sultan had witnessed the ever-more-hopeless battle. Saladin said 'No' before the exhausted swimmer's hair was dry. Just as the messenger was about to leap into the breakers again, Saladin looked up at the highest point of the city walls. First, the white flag was raised, and then a red one embroidered with three golden lions.

12

Richard was blood-besmirched and breathless, filthy and exhausted. He was still clutching his sword. Blood had congealed on its edge. Philip gave him some water. The French king's sword was in its scabbard.

'Are you hurt?' Philip asked. 'There are some knights from the Order of St John who can help if you're wounded.'

'We did it!' Richard cried. 'Aren't you happy? We've crushed the Saracens.'

'What shall we do with the prisoners?'

'How many are there?'

Philip reckoned aloud.

'Roughly two thousand seven hundred soldiers from Saladin's garrison in the city.'

'Others?'

Richard wiped blood and sand from his face with his hand. Philip handed him a kerchief he had under his mail.

'More than three hundred women and children.'

Richard handed the kerchief back.

'The women and children haven't taken part in the fighting,' Philip continued.

'Give orders for all the prisoners, soldiers, women and children to be roped together.'

'The women and children, too?'

Several knights and soldiers hurried to obey.

'Get back into formation. You'll be given orders shortly. We could be ambushed,' Richard yelled and waved them away.

Philip stood uneasily at Richard's side. Richard leant towards him and whispered.

'You heard what I said. All of them.'

'Why?' Philip replied.

'Give the order to de Sablé,' said Richard.

'Can't you see that Saladin is on the headland watching?' said Philip pointing.

'That doesn't diminish my power. Go to de Sablé. Now.'

Shortly afterwards Philip returned.

'Knight de Sablé asks whether there is any point in killing innocent women and children.'

'It's better to kill too many than too few!' Richard shouted. 'God will take care of the final selection.'

Several of the soldiers around them began to cheer.

'Does this conform to the ideals of chivalry?' Philip asked.

'Remember what the pope promised us. The greater the number we kill, the quicker we'll get to Paradise.'

Now is when it matters, Richard thought. He turned towards the promontory where Saladin was.

'Saladin! Can you hear me? I'll show you!'

With twenty-five men, knights and soldiers, Richard carried out his own orders.

Afterwards he rode back to Philip. His white horse was as gory as he was.

'Silence at last,' said Richard.

Philip was staring at the ground. Richard noticed that even de Sablé wouldn't meet his eye. Richard strode several horses' lengths away from Philip and glanced up at Acre's ruined walls without knowing what he was looking for.

Duke Leopold and all the other knights were summoned. Richard informed them that he would send a message to Saladin. He pointed in what Philip had said was the sultan's direction. He would demand that the sultan relinquish Ascalon immediately. In the course of only a few days the Crusaders would gain control of the entire coast northwards. After Ascalon, Jaffa and Haifa would be taken. It wouldn't take more than a couple of weeks. Then Jerusalem would be conquered and all infidels—Jews as well as Muslims—would be driven out or killed. The king, the duke and the knights around Richard cheered, raised their lances and swords and roared: 'Long live King Richard!'

Benny McGee, a knight from Aberdeen, sent an earthenware jar of brown liquor round the knights who sat on their horses in a ring round Richard. Duke Leopold of Austria was the only one who didn't want any.

'Here's tae us, an' whae's like us, dam few an' thir a' deid.'

'What's he saying?' Richard asked looking at Hubert Walter.

'It's Scots and means "Here's to us and people like us, there aren't many of them and they're all dead."'

Richard told his knights to pay careful attention. He had conceived a plan for the coming campaign right down to the smallest detail. Around the ring of knights stood their soldiers. Everyone supported Richard's notion of waiting before attacking. The only one who objected was Leopold.

The following day the duke came to Richard's tent and said that he wanted to leave the Holy Land. Richard shrugged his shoulders and decided to say as little as possible. As soon as the duke had left the tent, Richard asked Hubert Walter if he'd gone too far with him.

'By no means,' Walter replied. 'His forces really aren't crucial.'

Richard moved into the royal palace in Acre. The building was surrounded by eucalyptus trees whose pungent scent he couldn't get used to. But he loved the park and the area that had been turned into a fruit and vegetable garden. It was an oasis of green in the city, which had suffered the longest drought anyone could remember.

Richard ambled among the tall pear trees, gathered fruit, walked barefoot through the long grass and found a cabbage the gardener had missed. He placed it on a bench where the hard-working man would find it. One butterfly, and then another, flew restlessly around him. The flickering patches of yellow, black and red held his full attention. He noticed a flower he'd never seen. He got down on his stomach. The flower was beautiful, with blue petals. Richard couldn't decide whether it put him in mind of a delicate little creature begotten of sky and water, or a blue fire.

It was even hotter on the ground. Here and there the grass was scorched, even though this was one of the very few lawns in the city that was watered regularly. Richard dozed. He awoke with a start to discover a shadow behind him. The previous evening the knight Sir James Sheringham had told him that the Assassins would be trying their utmost to kill him. They were the enemies of both Saladin and the Crusaders. Their aim was chaos. They were unsurpassed at killing with a knife. Assassin killers were under the influence of hashish and were convinced that they would go straight to Paradise after they themselves were killed. Richard sprang up. The stranger ran. Most of the sun-beaten face was covered with a kerchief. Richard pulled his sword from its scabbard and gave chase. He quickly caught up with the fugitive and brought him down. Terrified, the skinny man stared at him with wan grey eyes, shook his head and said something Richard didn't understand. The face was that of the diligent gardener.

Richard gave de Sablé orders to take four officers and ride to Sultan Saladin with an invitation to discuss the terms for his surrender. It wasn't long before they were back. Saladin wouldn't meet the Crusaders' leader. Richard laughed. He wiped his face:

'The Devil has always been evil but never foolish. Doesn't he know that all the ports on the Mediterranean are about to fall? Surely he realizes what will happen to his people? If he'd played along, he might have saved a few thousand of them.'

'Saladin said more besides,' de Sablé went on.

'Speak.'

'He said that this time he wouldn't be as generous as when he conquered Jerusalem. He wouldn't show any mercy, he said.'

De Sablé was interrupted by laughter as he handed over a French translation of a letter from Saladin:

We will never surrender Ascalon. Do you really wish to spend the winter here, two months' journey from your family and your own country, you, a man in your prime who should be tasting the joys of life? I am in my own land, surrounded by all my children, grandchildren and those close to me. Allah will give one of us the victory. Dear King, you and your army must be wary of scorpions. Their bite can only be treated with the ash of burnt scorpions, herbs from the desert and mother's milk.

'Has he no more advice?' Richard demanded con-temptuously.

'Not at the moment,' de Sablé replied. 'Saladin invites the king and his men to dine with him, to pray at the Holy Sepulchre and visit the other Christian holy places.'

Richard was livid.

De Sablé asked, 'Why not accept the offer?'

It was hardly surprising that the Christians hadn't won when even the Grand Master of the Knights Templar had this sort of attitude. Didn't he realize just how wily the Devil was? He insinuated himself into all minds, even that of the Grand Master. It certainly wasn't a conscious act on de Sablé's part. His support from the beginning had been so genuine and wholehearted that the idea was unreasonable. But surely he knew, didn't he, that the Devil could seduce with smell, sight and sound, and make pious, gullible souls do his bidding? Couldn't he see the malicious intrigue?

'Don't you see that he'll kill me in an ambush?' Richard asked.

'No, I don't,' de Sablé replied in a calm voice. 'Neither Saladin or we gain anything by that.'

13

The map was spread out on Richard's writing table. On the left side of the parchment he could see the Mediterranean painted blue. The Kingdom of Jerusalem stretched from Gaza in the south to Tyre in the north. All the ports were marked with a pair of Devil's horns, Jerusalem was marked with three pairs. Tyre and Acre each had a cross by them.

Richard had summoned Philip and twelve of Philip's chief lieutenants. In addition, Walter and de Sablé were present to discuss how Ascalon was to be taken. Richard pointed at the map with his sword.

'Ascalon is of prime importance to us. Once Ascalon has fallen, the Holy City is only one day's ride away. And once that has been taken, the Saracens will no longer pollute towns like Ramallah, Nazareth and Bethlehem. The attack must come in the next few days, so that Saladin won't be able to regroup his army.'

The men nodded. Richard wondered why Philip seemed so uninterested.

Even after a lengthy dinner and quantities of wine Philip remained apathetic. Richard lamented the fact that after the victory the soldiers had been more interested in the women and wine in the city than in attacking Jerusalem. Philip made no answer.

Richard asked if it was Leopold's retreat that was worrying him. Philip shook his head.

'Even the finest of our men don't seem able to resist the temptation to debase themselves,' Richard said, hanging up the map of Ascalon.

'Soon our soldiers won't be able to stand for reveille,' said Baron Le Havre. 'We have to fetch them from the brothels.'

'There's something I have to tell you, Richard,' Philip said.

'You haven't been to the brothel, too?' Richard asked, laughing.

Philip looked at him for a long time before saying in a quiet voice:

'I've begun making preparations for sailing home.'

'Home?'

'We've taken Acre. That was a real feat, well, particularly your feat, Richard.'

Richard's face flushed. 'Our goal is Jerusalem.'

At first the French barons looked at each other in alarm, then turned to their king in amazement. The eldest, Raphael Dorin, said:

'You never mentioned this to us, Philip.'

They began arguing. Richard told them to stop, but to no avail.

'So now you're going home to steal the lands that belong to my mother and me?' Richard said finally. 'Please just go, Philip, so I won't have to see you again.'

'This war isn't exactly what we thought it would be, is it, Richard? Even the pope's got to admit that.'

'Go.'

'You all are witnesses. I swear I shall not attack any of King Richard's possessions or lands. In God's name.'

'This Crusade was far too great a challenge for you. I blame myself for putting my trust in you. You're a dwarf, Philip. It's only when a dwarf clambers up on to a large stage that you see just how small he is.'

Philip's face turned white. Sweat broke out on his brow. He stared at Richard for a moment before turning on his heel and walking out of the door, followed by his men.

As soon as they'd gone, de Sablé said that Philip's decision forced them to make a new plan. He suggested they delay the attack by a few days, until they'd received reinforcements. Richard noticed that he wasn't thinking clearly, anger had replaced the normal sober level-headedness he was so famed for in war.

'We ride for Ascalon tomorrow!'

After only seven weeks in Acre, Philip sailed for Messina. From there he journeyed to Rome to get the pope's blessing. The pope refused it. Three days later he was in Paris.

The following week Princess Joan and Queen Berengaria also left Acre with a large retinue. The queen's destination was Poitiers, where Eleanor was waiting.

Richard awoke in the middle of the night, bathed in sweat. He crept out of the tent in nothing but his nightclothes and arrived unnoticed behind a boulder among some dry scrub. His guards sat round a fire talking quietly as they fed the flames with dry branches from the surrounding thicket. Richard fell to his knees, clasped his hands and wept. He was angry with himself for not punishing Philip in front of his own knights for his treachery to God, the pope and himself. Richard had long entertained the hope that Philip would be his ally until the day Jerusalem was retaken. He had believed that Philip wouldn't give way to the weaknesses in his character. How could he have been so naive about Philip? He'd hoped they would draw closer together. Was anything more dangerous than placing your trust in another human being? Philip had betrayed him more than anyone else, because Richard had once esteemed him so highly. Rage and remorse caused the kneeling figure to tremble. He raised his folded hands and prayed to God for a sign or a word as to what he should do.

He wiped away his tears, got up as silently as he could and made sure the pickets hadn't noticed him before stealing back to his tent. What a curse it was to start asking questions. Where did they come from? They hadn't yet managed to paralyze him but, if he allowed them to go on hatching in his head like vipers' eggs, they would sap the strength of his arms and legs. His movements would become hesitant, the lethal slashes with the sword would turn into half-hearted hacks that would at best injure the enemy.

Could the pope have misunderstood God? Was it really true that the more Saracens you killed the faster you got to Paradise? Did that include women and children, could he really be quite certain? Had the pope heard properly when God was addressing him? Hubert Walter had once said that the pope was hard of hearing.

In the mornings, Richard mounted Acre's ruined city wall and stared out across the sea to where his own royal ship had arrived at the head of his fleet four weeks ago. He preferred not to look at the sea rocks near the shore in front of the city walls and fortress. It had taken weeks before the blood of the executions he had led was washed away. The sight of the water, the breakers, the unending blue, the haze, made him forget. Blue, nothing but blue all the way to the horizon, no colour was more lovely. It covered seabed and sea spectres. The endless motion of the waves, the sound of the water slapping against rocks, its hiss could remove the discontent of being himself and make him part of the horizon that reached to his neck. He looked down to the shore. Morning there was like the first morning of the world. And in the middle of the day, at its zenith, when the sun hammered down on the anvil of the sea, when the heat was intolerable, a flying fish or two might distract him from his worries. In the evenings the colours became darker and the outlines sharper, the sea turned deep blue and the beach golden yellow. But best of all were the nights, when it was cool at last and everything was black, apart from the cliffs that were whitewashed by moonlight. Then he could hear the rhythm of the waves even more clearly, like some great, timeless heart into which he dissolved and became a part.

14

'You knights, Davenport and Sheringham, keep close by my side. Cover me. I'll ride in front,' was all Richard managed to say before he was struck by a stone from a sling.

He came to himself lying in his full armour in the dust. He coughed, was it blood? His right eye was caked and shut. He could see with his left one. What would he have given for a drop of water? His three kingdoms and the blue heavens he was beginning to glimpse a little more of. The pain. If only he could pass out. He could hardly move. Where was his horse? It was lying by his side. Blood was pouring from its muzzle. It was caked in blood and all that dust. It must have been dead some time. He called out to the others. No one answered.

He remembered that his forces had had the upper hand but something must have gone wrong. Had he been hit? Was his neck bleeding? He tried to rub the blood and dust from his eyes and face. Was it his blood? Yes, his neck was bleeding. He tried to get on to his hands and knees. Round about him were low houses made of earth and sand. But where were the soldiers? Where was the enemy? He couldn't get on to his side. His armour was too heavy. There was no one to be seen but he could hear the battle raging a little way off. Saladin's men must have managed to drive away the men fighting at his side. Now he remembered—his horse, the best of the three, had received three arrows to its neck. It had fallen without a single stagger. So was this how it was to end?

Imagine if his mother could see him now. His mother who'd been so certain that he could neither lose nor die in the Holy Land. Would he have wished her to see him in this state? So that she might understand just how wrong she'd been? He knew that, more than anything, she'd have wanted to take his place, lying there in the dust, waiting for death, so that he might live. That was what she was like.

Again he tried to wipe his face so that he could see better.

On the horizon . . . weren't there people there? Weren't they some of the local people? He asked God to give him strength. It must be some of Saladin's men. A stoop-shouldered man was helped down from his horse. Surely, it was impossible? Richard blinked several times. Yes, it really was him. From the description de Sablé had given, it must be Saladin.

'What triumph you must feel to see me lying like this,' Richard shouted.

One of Richard's soldiers came running. The young man looked across at Saladin's archers. They were aiming at Richard. The soldier threw himself down to cover his king.

Richard heard a shouted order. The bows were drawn. The archers looked at their leader. They were waiting for the next order.

There was another shout, even louder.

The bows were lowered.

Saladin took one of his stallions and gave it a tap across the rump, so that it trotted in Richard's direction. The exhausted soldier grabbed the reins and hitched the horse to an abandoned cart.

'What's happening?' Richard asked.

'Saladin himself has saved us, Sire! Saved us! We've lost thousands but he's let us go.'

The soldier managed to divest Richard of all his armour, until he lay in his under garments, still clothed in chain mail. He was sweaty, filthy and beaten black and blue. His right leg felt as if it was broken.

'Why didn't they kill us?' said the soldier.

After several attempts he got Richard to his feet. Richard saw the corpses of his men around him before his right leg gave way and he collapsed into the dust again. Now he caught the stink. Through his mouth and nostrils came the smell of bodies, blood and excrement. Armless and headless corpses lay strewn about him. The dead horses' heads and necks were full of arrows. A number of the men in armour had succumbed to Greek fire. The burning oil and brimstone had overpowered them. Richard recognized some of the men from the arms painted on the shields or lances that lay close to their corpses. Here, close by him, lay Davenport's shield, and there the helmet he'd managed to tear off before death claimed him. His face was in the sand, Richard turned the head and looked at it. Just next to it lay the remains of Sheringham. His hair and mouth were recognizable. They had sacrificed themselves for him, the Crusaders' king, God's Sword.

'I'm not worth it, do you hear?' Richard yelled.

'Sire, we must get away. Put your right arm round my neck and I'll see if I can get you on to the horse. These Arab horses are smaller than ours, eh?'

Was there anything less interesting than the size of a horse? Had the soldier said it to make him concentrate less on the pain and the sight of the dead? The houses, the sand beneath him, the sky, his right hand, it was on his arm, he didn't know in which direction they should ride, everything meant equally much, or little, to him. All hope does, he thought, is enable us to suffer a little longer.

Richard began to tremble.

'Almighty God, why do you permit our finest men to come to this?'

He stared at a charred corpse in a suit of armour.

'Where were you, God? Weren't you on our side?'

He slumped forwards on the horse's back, with one arm around its neck. The other gripped its black mane tightly. The soldier held the reins and supported Richard as best he could.

Two days later Richard gathered his generals in his tent. No one, not even Walter or de Sablé, mentioned the fact that that Richard had almost been killed during the battle.

Richard began by saying that he had no intention of giving up Ascalon. The men nodded. A scout interrupted the meeting with reports that Saladin seemed to be pulling his army back from Ascalon and Jaffa in order to strengthen the defence of Jerusalem. Richard gave orders that if so, Ascalon and Jaffa were to be occupied.

De Sablé rolled out the map and marked the towns of Arson, Ascalon and Jaffa with crosses. He believed it was difficult to control the ports and attack Jerusalem simultaneously. Control of the ports on the Mediterranean was essential for getting supplies from Europe. These included men and weapons which were most often shipped from Messina in Italy.

De Sablé thought they would need more than four hundred thousand men to command the coast. They had a quarter of this number at most, and if they took Jerusalem they risked letting the ports fall back into the hands of Saladin. According to de Sablé, it was like a stalemate in chess. Walter shared his opinion. Richard said nothing. He realized that Philip's retreat had weakened them considerably and that Saladin's army had shown itself to be much stronger than he'd imagined. Saladin had rescued him in the battle at Ascalon, as if he were some small child who needed protecting. Richard glanced quickly at the men around him. How much had de Sablé and Walter found out about the incident? If Saladin had killed him, he would have become a martyr and gone to Heaven. Why had Saladin let him live? So that his allies would realize that Richard wasn't invincible? It was a stratagem, it hadn't simply been prompted by decency. Why didn't God lessen the heat? Richard glanced across at de Sablé and Walter several times. They looked irresolute. Did they doubt his strength?

15

Richard could spot the dust cloud from the horses a long way off. He went into his tent, smoothed back his hair, sheathed his sword and seated himself in the largest of the five chairs, the one that most resembled a throne. He was waiting for Saladin's brother, al-Adil. Richard had agreed to meet him after al-Adil had promised that their conversation would be informal and merely 'hint at a few solutions'. A few days earlier Saladin had refused to meet Richard outside Jerusalem. 'Occupying forces have no right to dictate to me. My brother is my representative,' the messenger had repeated.

Richard felt his right leg. He could certainly feel that the leg wasn't as strong as it had been but it had healed fast. He couldn't rid himself of the idea that possibly Saladin had saved his life because he needed him. Could it be that it was easier for Saladin to mobilize his own people when Richard was leading the Crusaders? After the deaths of Count Renauld and Frederik I Barbarossa, he was the only one left who was spoken of with fear and respect by the Saracens.

On the table before him lay a cylinder of leather. Inside was the letter which the three messengers had risked their lives to carry, across the Alps, via Rome to

Messina, and from there by ship to Gaza, until they reached Richard's headquarters a short distance from the town of Jericho. He loved the name of the town and repeated it aloud to himself. Saladin controlled Jericho with a small force to keep it open to all religions and to secure free trade. Richard had never been further from his homeland.

He rose abruptly, took a couple of long strides to the tent opening and peered out. There was no one in sight. He turned on his heel and fetched the leather container. He wanted to read the first paragraph again before al-Adil arrived. Richard unfurled the papyrus roll.

> *Dear son, my own Richard, you must know that each day I wait to hear that you have taken Jerusalem. How I shall rejoice when Philip learns that the Holy City is conquered. He will have to crawl on his knees from Rouen to the Church of the Holy Sepulchre and beg for your mercy. Only promise me not to give up . . .*

Richard read the letter's concluding lines:

> *The poem 'Fire and Water' is both good and beautiful. I was right in that matter too, you see. You could be a fine poet, my son.*

He heard sounds and looked out.

Al-Adil was at the head of an escort of twenty. They were riding at a fast gallop. Just before they came to the first tent, seven of Richard's soldiers appeared. It took a long time for the dust to settle. Al-Adil gave orders to his men to remain in the saddle until he returned. One of his adjutants held his horse's reins, while he was led, alone, to Richard's tent. At the tent flap he was searched.

'It doesn't take a long knife-blade to kill a man,' al-Adil said in Arabic and French to the soldiers and smiled.

When he entered, Richard was standing, studying a map of Jerusalem which had been set up on an easel in front of his chair.

'Good King, don't pretend you haven't noticed that I'm here,' said al-Adil.

'I've noticed how short the distance is from here to Jerusalem,' said Richard calmly.

'You're keen on poetry, aren't you?'

Richard shrugged, straightened and invited al-Adil to sit down at the table which was spread with mutton, olives, bread and fruit.

Al-Adil had brought poetry with him, four Persian and two Arabic poems from Saladin, translated into French. Richard knew nothing of Omar Khayyam or al-Fahr. They were supposed to be negotiating. Not discussing poetry. Had Saladin and his brother lost their wits?

Saladin had sent an accompanying letter in which he said: 'Remember, brave King, in love and poetry Allah has given us a glimpse of Heaven.' Al-Adil mentioned several of the Moorish and French poets that Richard's half-sister Marie and her husband also admired. Al-Adil asked Richard if he knew their poems. Richard nodded.

'How is your health, Majesty?'

'Excellent.'

'You are not well. Have you got typhus?'

'You're not a doctor.'

'I have read the works of the learned Ibn Sina, the one you call Avicenna. I also have some friends who are doctors. I can summon the best physicians there are from Damascus. Hasn't Adelard of Bath translated al-Qanum, the Arabic medical text, into your language?'

'Get to the point,' Richard said irritably.

'Isn't it strange how anxious we are that those we perceive as enemies should not show us kindness?'

'Don't pretend that you and your brother haven't got ulterior motives.'

'We hope you will realize that our faith and our people are not what the pope has taught you.'

'Showing people kindness is as dangerous as kissing wild animals,' said Richard crassly.

'May I bring along two of my doctors one day soon?' al-Adil asked. 'It will be done with the utmost discretion.'

Richard hesitated.

'If you die, brave King, complete chaos will descend and no one will benefit from that. This is a disease your own doctors have little or no experience of.'

Richard had hoped that the talks would take a more substantial turn the following day. He was surprised when al-Adil really did turn up with the doctors he'd promised. The elder was called Ibn Maymun. He quickly concluded that Richard had typhus.

He wore a skullcap. Richard turned to al-Adil.

'Is he a Jew?'

The doctor smiled. Al-Adil made no reply.

Ibn Maymun pressed his fingers to Richard's wrist and neck, before examining the king's mouth and throat with a spatula. He took several ointments and herbs out of a leather satchel he'd brought with him. Richard let him rub the ointments on his throat and temples. But when he was told to swallow an infusion of herbs, he refused. He looked across at al-Adil and said that this reminded him of what Hildegard of Bingen prescribed. Before al-Adil could answer, the doctor said that Hildegard had learnt most of her medicine in al-Andalus. After that, Richard swallowed the herbal mixture.

When the consultation was over, al-Adil repeated Saladin's invitation to visit the Church of the Holy Sepulchre and have dinner with him. Richard again refused the invitation, even though his aide tried to protest.

As al-Adil was about to leave, he placed a hand on Richard's shoulder and looked him in the eye.

'Do you know what my brother and I call you?'

'No.'

'King Richard the Lionheart. Because we recognize you for a brave and courageous general. And because you are treated like a lion by those you lead. I do not understand all that is in your heart, but you are the only leader we can and wish to deal with.'

'It's very hot. Do you know where I can bathe?'

'I recommend the Dead Sea. One floats even if one cannot swim.'

'I can swim extremely well,' said Richard emphatically.

Once al-Adil and his entourage had left, Richard decided that there really was something in their nickname for him, and a smile spread across his face.

'Is anyone else coming for a bathe?' he shouted to his two servants.

He didn't wait for an answer.

Shouldn't he be glad to be alive, that his leg was better and that his typhus, according to the doctor, would soon be cured?

Richard and his servants rode the short distance from Jericho to the Dead Sea. The lake was surrounded by an arid landscape of sand, rocks and desiccated shrubs. The servants stood on the shore and stared. He laughed and splashed his arms. His penis pointed straight up to the heavens. The men on the shore looked at each other, giggled and shook their heads.

From where he lay floating in the deep blue water, Richard could see high, domed mountains without a single tree. The water contained no fish and not a hint of marine life.

Sodom and Gomorra once lay at the southern end of the Dead Sea. It didn't surprise him. Here and there he could see small clusters of salt pillars. Richard saw no birds. Perhaps God loved the birds so dearly that he made the trees, he thought.

The Dead Sea lay hundreds of cubits lower than the Mediterranean. According to the scholars, this was the spot on the earth that lay furthest from the sun. Richard pointed to his sunburnt belly and shouted to the men ashore that it didn't look like it.

On his way home, Richard wanted to ride into Jericho market. One of his servants asked if this were advisable, considering that the town was under Saladin's control. Richard replied that the sultan's forces kept it open to all.

He bought two apricots. Richard walked with his escort and squinted at the sun. Its heat made him curl his upper lip and show his teeth. On the edge of the market he could see dusty, spiky acacia trees and palms with green and dusty-grey crowns that waved just perceptibly. The ground was as dry as a biblical desert. The low, white houses were polished by the winds and rain of winter. The plaster was patchy or completely missing.

He caught the smell of fresh bread. Was it possible to buy some? In one corner of the market he saw a woman holding up a loaf. She was standing with five other women. She was surprisingly light-skinned, with rust-brown freckles. If he hadn't known better he might have taken her for a Christian woman from Anjou or Normandy. The thought confused him. He'd imagined that Saracens would have been more obviously different. Richard stood watching the women and the loaves for a long time. The smell of the baking seeped into his nostrils. The women stroked and patted the loaves, occasionally tossing them in the air and shouting the price. One of his servants smiled and asked Richard if he didn't agree that the women were beautiful. Richard shook his head. The men smiled at one another.

To get back to the entrance to the market where their horses were tethered, Richard and his escort had to pass through an alley. He got separated from his servants. Emaciated beggars stretched out hands. Some of them were leprous. Several had suppurating sores. Disgust welled up within him. He heard muttering.

Here, in the world's oldest town, Richard thought, God must have planned that men should learn to live in close proximity. And when they went astray, he would guide and forgive them. Caesar, Herod and Alexander the Great had palaces here, with the best wells. The earth was red, then as now, the rock almost pink. Jericho must have been one great oasis then. The plants and trees had found new life in the setting sun, the Virginia creeper's red leaves and the violet hues of the iris captured all attention. Was it in this town that God had witnessed what men were capable of? Was it here he'd begun to regret creating them?

Soon he found himself in the midst of an undulating mass, with beggars on all sides. They cared nothing for his uniform or sword. He was driven forwards from side to side. He had great difficulty keeping his balance. They clutched at his feet, his legs, his thighs and his cloak. They had nothing to lose. If he'd drawn his sword they wouldn't have worried. They blessed every part of his body, pointed up at heaven to elicit Allah's attention to any small change he might bestow. All about him, the confused faces, shafts of bone, crutches, the foul-smelling clothes, the sweating heads, all became one noisy plea. It was impossible to get away.

By some accident, or rather out of heedlessness, he happened to look the almost fair, native woman in the eyes, the pupils, the whites of her eyes, the shape of them, he tried to push, he didn't want to see anyone, he shouted, in a language they didn't understand, he had to look into those eyes again, they were green, their colour was, yes, not entirely unlike his own, he was drowning, he was being choked. He had hacked several hundred people to death single-handedly at Acre. If only they'd known that, as they pressed shamelessly up against him, as if he were a nobody. Had any of them fled from Acre? Had the green-eyed woman made clothes for him in Anger, his favourite town? Of course she hadn't—but what a resemblance.

Richard's hand grabbed the horsewhip he'd pushed into his belt, and he let fly at the natives around him. The alley was too narrow and the crowd too great.

'Be off with you!' he roared. 'I'll strike deeper and harder!'

It was one of the most unpleasant things Richard had experienced. This was far more terrifying than being in battle.

Only when Richard began to wield his sword did the throng move aside.

16

A small contingent from Richard's army had occupied the summit of the Mount of Olives. Richard was surprised that Saladin had allowed it to happen without attacking. Presumably this was because there were only three hundred men. The main force of almost twenty thousand was camped at the town of Tyre. The Holy City lay below, just out of range of bow and arrow and crossbow.

All around him in the scrub were wild roses, white, heavy with water, juicy as fruit. Close by he saw large nectar-filled flowers with violet petals. The sun was lifting the haze from the last light shower. He moved through a gossamer thin cloud and knew that the sun was shining above it and would soon disperse the dot of mist around him. The outline of the nearest bushes became steadily clearer. There, on the Mount of Olives, with the Holy City in the distance, it became clear to the English king that if he were to take the city, it had to be now. Some might call this a desperate strategy. But he had experience of surprising his enemies and attacking when they least expected it.

Richard had been in the Holy Land for a year and three months. Everything had defied his expectations—heat, sand, dust, breath, thirst, the enemy's military capabilities, the cunning of the Saracens, the problems with supplies from Europe, especially Messina. But most difficult of all was that Saladin had proved quite a different general to what he'd expected. In addition, the sultan was fighting in terrain he knew.

But it was a fact that he'd never been so close to his goal as now—it was within sight. Large parts of Saladin's forces were engaged in battles south of Jaffa, against an almost similarly sized Crusader army.

This was the sixth continuous month of futile tactics. The pattern was always the same. If one side pulled its forces in the direction of Acre, Tyre, Jaffa or Haifa, the enemy followed, but without any obvious military gain. One thing was certain, though—because of the battles on the coast, Saladin was able to control Jerusalem.

Everyone turned to him about everything, and he didn't know what to say. He hated that. He, whom God had chosen, must surely have an answer? He'd believed that God would reveal himself to him several times and show the way. It hadn't happened. And his mother hadn't come to visit, as he'd expected her to.

Richard looked at the path that snaked gently down the valley between him and Jerusalem. The sky was blue and the clouds white. He was waiting for Robert de Sablé and two of his knights. After much discussion, Richard had given de Sablé permission to go to Saladin. De Sablé thought it could do no harm. If one took some of the heat out of the conflict it would be possible, when Saladin imagined that the Crusaders were more tractably disposed, to strike later on.

Richard had labelled them 'brothers in ignorance'. He scanned the path, feeling more and more certain that he should never have given way.

He was unsure if the scent in the air came from the cypresses or the carob trees. A donkey loaded with olives trudged towards him. Its driver wasn't visible. Perhaps he was hidden behind the slowly moving, four-legged toiler? The earth it walked on was ruddy and the sun had shone long enough for all the moisture to have evaporated.

His hands were sweating. They were covered with flies. He clapped his palms together. A little pile of black and grey, with the occasional wing stirring, lay at his feet. His boots, his worn jerkin and homespun breeches were the same as he'd worn in the field. As were his belt and sword. But apart from that it was impossible to tell he was a Crusader, far less their leader. Richard began to think about a poem Saladin had given him. He couldn't recall the name of the poet but al-Adil had translated the words for him. The first line went: 'My dread is deep.' Al-Adil had added that: '"My dread" refers to Allah, the one you call God.' The rest of the poem went:

> *I have made this world.*
> *How well it looks!*
> *What shall I do?*
> *My dread is deep and my stars*
> *are far too far away*
> *to comfort me.*

Richard repeated the lines: 'My dread is deep and my stars are far too far away.'

Surely de Sablé and his knights would be back soon?

It wouldn't be long before night spread itself over them all—enemy and friend, infidel and believer, jackal and lamb, thorn bush and olive tree.

Saladin had doubtless tempted them with fair words and killed them afterwards. That shouldn't be a surprise to anyone. In that case, the three simpletons had got what they deserved. He was the last man on earth to feel sorry for their witless act. If Saladin tried to hand over their bodies, he would refuse to accept them.

He was hungry and was just about to turn back to camp when the sound of hooves reached him. He peered down the valley. De Sablé rode in front. Should he hide? Or pretend that he just happened to be out?

The three knights were surprised to see Richard alone.

'You weren't worried about us?'

Richard shook his head.

'You've been drinking wine, I can smell it.'

'It was quite an experience to kneel in the Church of the Holy Sepulchre,' de Sablé said.

The others nodded.

'And that strange, holy light,' de Sablé went on, 'and the sounds, the reflection and the banquet with Saladin. He barely reached to my chest.'

'Was he ill?'

'He was very thin.'

'Will he die soon?' Richard asked.

They looked at one another doubtfully. De Sablé shook his head.

'What a meal, masses of grilled lamb and chicken, saffron-coloured rice, salads, fruit, figs, dates, raisins as large as nuts . . . and the palace, it wasn't big but it was elegant.'

'We've got enough food here,' Richard put in. 'And you think you're in a state to fight him now? You've been ruined.'

'We're wilier than Saladin.'

Richard could tell that de Sablé really meant it and was about to ask how he could be so certain. De Sablé asked if Richard wished to borrow his horse. The Templars' Grand Master said that he would walk the last stretch to the tents, but Richard shook his head emphatically, he knew quite well that de Sablé was trying to humour him. When the others were out of earshot, he asked what impression Saladin had made on de Sablé.

'Generous and scholarly. By the way . . .'

De Sablé indicated the leather pouch on his horse's back.

'. . . I've brought a new typhus medicine for you from his court physician.'

'Give it to me.'

De Sablé fished out a small earthenware bottle. Richard tore it out of his hand and hurled the bottle against a flat stone on the path in front of them. Hubert Walter came riding out from the tents.

'What's afoot, Sire?'

'De Sablé and Walter! I will not take medicine from an infidel. At dawn I want fifty of our best soldiers drawn up here. They will accompany me on an attack that will surprise the enemy. There'll be no horses and they won't be wearing armour.'

'I volunteer,' said de Sablé.

'I said I wanted our *best* soldiers. Not those who sit down at table with the enemy. Get me a detailed map of Saladin's palace. The soldiers must be picked from those we have here on the Mount of Olives. We can't get any from the main force or the sultan's elite Turkish troops will notice. They keep a close watch on our movements.'

'Understood, but promise us one thing—if it fails we'll pull out of the Holy Land temporarily and raise another, more suitable, army.'

'It's a promise,' said Richard and looked at Walter.

'You seem certain that the plan will work, Sire,' Walter said.

Richard nodded.

Next evening at midnight, fifty-one men left the tented camp. They were disguised as Arab traders. The only things they carried, outside their tunics, were goatskin bags of water. Under them they had ropes and knives. They were to be back before dawn. Richard was certain that the men who were with him would succeed in their task. They reached the city walls unobserved. They were divided into five groups. Four of them contained ten men each. Richard's numbered eleven. He gave detailed orders to the group leaders. With the aid of their ropes they scaled the wall. De Sablé's map of the heart of Jerusalem proved accurate. Close to the sultan's palace Richard gathered the four other leaders and gave his final orders. All was quiet around them. For an instant the clouds that covered the moon parted. Richard saw the men's eager eyes. Soon they would murder Saladin and his immediate family. Richard asked if any of them wanted to turn back, for nothing was more dangerous than soldiers who were gripped with fear. They all shook their heads. Richard said that they were God's and his trusted elite force. Just then a net fell and covered them. Richard began to lash out round him until he fell. The men ended up in a pile, on top of one another. Struggling, Richard was dragged away from them.

Not a word was said to him as he was bound and searched.

'What are you going to do with my men?' Richard asked the person he took to be commanding Saladin's household troops.

'The sultan has been waiting for you,' he answered in French. 'Your men will be freed once you have left for your own country. My men will set you loose by the tent you slept in last night. Farewell.'

Richard was blindfolded. A cloth was held under his nose and he fell asleep. He awoke next morning in his own tent without the ropes or blindfold. Richard ran out of his tent towards his guards, who'd been certain he was still in Jerusalem. They asked where his soldiers were, Richard replied that they'd be coming back sometime soon. He wasn't lying, he just wanted to take in the truth bit by bit. If he'd related it all accurately, he thought, the army would lose the last remnant of its fighting spirit.

17

It was the last Sunday of September 1192. Richard requested Stephen of Turnham to report to the king's tent as soon as possible, a quarter day's march from the walls of Arsuf. Richard and Turnham were to lay the final plans for the conquest of the city. The young knight could not understand why the king's mood was so bad. Only after a meal and a convincing argument that the victory was close at hand did Richard relax. He asked if Turnham wanted wine. The knight hesitated. Richard said it was an order. After the third glass the king related that de Sablé and Walter had just visited him and asked if he were going to keep his promise about retreating. When Turnham asked what this all meant, he wouldn't answer. Instead, Richard said that he dreamt more and more often of the places where he'd enjoyed riding, in his own Angevin lands.

'But that's a pleasant experience, surely?' Turnham said encouragingly.

'I'm usually riding in Gascony, in the far south, often with the Pyrenees behind me, with Montauban to the north and Toulouse in the east. I love that rolling countryside.'

'Then why should it be so bad to dream about it?'

'Do you remember King Philip's flight?'

'You said he was a traitor because he put his own interests before those placed on us by God and the pope.'

'You remember well, Turnham.'

Richard began to pace round the large wooden chair Turnham was sitting in. On the floor was a shaggy, circular, black-and-white carpet of monkey skin. The tent contained two tables. A larger one, with room for four people, and a smaller, supporting a chessboard. The board and pieces were made of green and white onyx, the table and chairs of teak. The walls of the tent were of whitish-grey canvas. Other knights had tapestries, pictures or decorations on their tent walls. There was only one thing Richard wanted on his wall. Above his bed, which was enclosed in netting to protect him from insects, hung the map that showed in detail which towns had been taken and where the Crusading forces were.

'I'm convinced Philip arrived at his sinful decision after he began dreaming of the landscapes he remembers with greatest fondness, those he looks back on, from his childhood, those he regards as his own.'

'And which are they?'

'Rouen.'

'And you're sure of that?'

'I am. The Devil is cunning. He works his way into our minds, gets hold of things we consider our own and uses them as his evil bait. Do you understand?'

'Not entirely.'

'First there is the thought that reminds you of your own childhood, provided it was as happy as Philip's, and then comes the second thought, which we add to the first one, the thought that because we are kings of realms and peoples, these domains are ours, domains we own on behalf of our people and never give up. We protect their borders and defend them. It is what our subjects expect of us. But in this war, here in the Holy Land, this is the most sinful of all thoughts for a king or a knight, because God has entrusted us with a mission.'

'There's no doubt about that, Richard,' Turnham said before drawing breath and adding, 'But what does your beginning to dream about Gascony mean?'

His words didn't sound malicious. Rather, they had the ring of honest innocence.

Richard regretted being confidential. The servant asked if they wanted more wine. Richard said no at once, without looking at Turnham.

'Do you know what I said to Robert de Sablé last evening?' Richard asked.

He was putting his boots on to go out. 'That my motto will be *Dieu et mon droit.*'

'God and my right,' repeated Stephen of Turnham.

Saladin drew a large part of his forces towards Ramallah, a day's journey from Jerusalem, and continued to strengthen the defences in and around the Holy City. The Crusaders had taken Jaffa, the port closest to Jerusalem, three days away. Richard took ten thousand men to Jaffa to maintain the defence of the city.

Richard sat in a park on one of Jaffa's hills. He gazed at the white houses on the slopes round the harbour. The flowers and trees had long since wilted. He tried to imagine what the palms, roses, orange trees and rhododendron bushes would look like after the rains came. He could glimpse what had once been the teeming market in the town's centre, with vegetables and fruit of every conceivable variety and colour. So, under normal circumstances, surely, it must be the Mediterranean's loveliest city, Richard thought as he sat in the shade of a jacaranda tree.

Earlier that day he'd received bleak reports. When he wasn't in charge personally, the soldiers were increasingly taking liberties. This lack of morals was destroying God's army from within. The soldiers robbed the conquered towns and villages, didn't pay what they owed at the brothels, raped Christian women and plundered shops and inns. Indeed, even here and in Arsuf, a little to the north, much the same thing happened.

More of the wells known to the Crusaders had been poisoned by the locals. Richard was annoyed with himself for failing to foresee that this might happen. With each day that passed, he and his men had less water to drink. Earlier in the day he'd ordered greater firmness in torturing the natives, to get them to say where their water came from. Half a day had passed and he hadn't learnt that anyone had given away a single drop.

Richard sat and looked out across the Mediterranean. Blue waves, breeze, weren't there any foam crests out there? It was as if he were staring through water. He could hear, couldn't he? There were sounds round him? He saw seagulls.

He let his gaze wander over the houses that stood at the top of the ridge. They clung to the slope. The market was there, among the houses. The gulls flapped, they didn't fall. He looked at his hands. Each hand had five fingers. He hadn't lost a single one. He conjured up his mother's eyes, her curly hair. His wrists were pale and cold, despite all the heat. His chest and armpits sweated. He felt nauseous. He looked at the sea. The waves taunted him with water and foam. The sky fell down and folded itself about him. Everything went white. Richard fell on his side.

18

Two of the household guard had carried him back to his tent. Al-Adil was to visit him that evening. He lay on his bed all afternoon. In the evening he seated himself at his writing table. He propped his head on one hand and dozed. First the camel disappeared beneath him, a palm tree shot up into the sky and then the moon fell and rolled at his feet. But what had replaced the camel? It was something a lot larger. Slowly he realized it was a whale that was riding up and over hills of seaweed through the murmuring waters of sleep.

Suddenly al-Adil was standing in front of him holding out a carafe.

'You will never have tasted better water. Try it.'

Richard grasped the carafe and gulped down half the contents.

'You were really thirsty.'

Richard caught his breath and dried his mouth.

'Give us back the Holy Cross of Christ. We know you've hidden it in Jerusalem. It belongs to us Christians.'

'My brother and I are not sure that your men are capable of looking after it. Does the Cross mean so much to you? Doesn't the life your men are leading in our towns indicate that they are thinking of anything but the Cross of Jesus?'

Neither of them mentioned the abortive attack on Jerusalem.

Al-Adil presented Richard with ice for his fever, green and black grapes and honey from the area around Beirut, which, according to al-Adil should be consumed 'for health and for enjoyment'. He'd brought a peace proposal, translated into French, which had been approved by Saladin. Richard said not a word about the gifts but took the document from al-Adil and began to read. A servant collected the presents and carried them to an adjacent tent.

'You are not yourself today. Perhaps you have got worse, Majesty?'

'I dream about Gascony,' Richard exclaimed.

'I'm glad to hear it,' said al-Adil.

Richard read the document several times. His mouth went dry and he felt nauseous.

The agreement gave the ports to the Crusaders, apart from Jaffa. Jerusalem would remain in Saladin's hands. Pilgrims would be able to visit the Holy City, which Saladin had allowed since he'd conquered it, and the Cross would be handed over under certain conditions. Richard studied the French text carefully. He stared across at al-Adil, who calmly kept looking straight ahead. The two of them were alone. It had been Richard's wish.

If *I* can't take Jerusalem, Richard thought, who else could? The world cannot move on while Jerusalem is in Saracen hands. Because of him, everything that was good, genuine, best for humanity, would stop at the walls of the

Holy City. Could God possibly forgive him? How lonely God must have been when he created human beings. Had the Lord regretted it? Would he understand that Richard had no choice? He must cling to the hope that he would return better prepared. God must listen to him, if only this once.

Richard told al-Adil that he needed some air. It was even hotter outside. He vomited, came back and sat down. What was this he was about to do? What would Eleanor say? She would be furious. Wouldn't she? But she knew perfectly well that victory often comes by indirect means. He would have liked to talk to her so much. Surely *she'd* realize he had no choice, even if God didn't?

He had promised Walter and de Sablé that he'd leave for home. A knight kept his word. If his forces didn't retreat, they risked being annihilated. Sweat soaked his hair, his beard and his face, he glanced down at his hands, sweat seeped out between the knuckles of his middle and index fingers. When he'd come ashore at Acre, he hadn't realized that the heat was the sultan's invisible army. An army which was everywhere, which was impervious to lances or catapults, which forced its way into nostrils, mouth, throat, lungs, which put a puissant hand around his heart and squeezed a bit harder every day. Richard tried to breathe more slowly. Al-Adil seemed unaffected. Richard could see no sign of moisture on his face.

'Do you want something to drink?' Richard asked and nodded towards the carafe in front of them.

'No, thank you, I am not thirsty,' said al-Adil.

'I'm not either,' said Richard.

Richard was grateful that his mother couldn't see him. Was al-Adil smiling? Was there a small twitch at the corners of his lips? Saladin's brother placed the quill between them.

'Will you sign first, Majesty?'

'No,' said Richard.

Al-Adil wrote his own and his brother's name in both Arabic and Latin script.

Surely Eleanor would understand that if they'd carried on they might risk losing everything? Now they could return and win the final battle for Jerusalem. Al-Adil mustn't think this would be the last time they'd see each other. He was about to open his mouth and say this. Richard lifted his head and looked across at al-Adil. He was bareheaded. The silk scarf that had been tied round his head when he'd ridden up, lay by his side. His beard was short and well groomed. His black hair was also short. His face was relaxed. He looked as if he had plenty of time. Provided he understood this was just a temporary withdrawal. They would soon meet again. Then he would be better prepared, Saladin and al-Adil would lose Jerusalem for good.

He wrote quickly. The quill hardly scratched the parchment.

'Richard I,' he wrote.

19

Richard summoned his knights to a meeting just before sunrise. On the horizon he could make out a stripe of violet. It was cold. Two fires were lit. A soldier banged on a cooking pot to chase away the poisonous tarantulas. The spiders were attracted by the warmth of the fires. Richard studied the knights thoroughly as they arrived sleepily, looking perplexed.

'Didn't you sleep last night, Richard?' Walter asked. 'Why all this hurry?'

If Richard's closest companions turned against him everything would be lost. He couldn't postpone it any longer. He had to explain what he'd done the night before, that he'd signed, alone, to save them the unpleasantness, as he was in overall command. He mustn't hesitate but speak clearly and openly. He had to make them believe that he'd never been so sure and decisive.

But what if they said he'd failed? God had placed confidence in him and commanded him to lead the crusading army. They trusted him, just as Jesus had trusted Judas. Was it God who'd ordained that he'd get no closer to Jerusalem than Gethsemane, where Jesus was betrayed?

The men stood in a circle round him, in full uniform. All were carrying their best swords. Richard chose to let his eyes rest on Walter, who had supported him when he'd urged the knights not to visit Saladin.

Richard lifted his voice and portrayed the peace agreement as a partial victory. They had to retreat temporarily, not rapidly, but over a period of months, possibly longer. At home they must build up a large, new, loyal army.

He spoke more rapidly than usual.

'We need an army that can annihilate the Saracens. Thank you for your bravery when traitors like King Philip and Duke Leopold left us, just when we needed to stand together.'

When he'd finished speaking, he turned his gaze away from Walter's seemingly calm face, to the knights who'd been incensed when King Philip had departed. Now they seemed uncertain. Walter took the floor. He said it was a sensible decision.

'On occasion, the world's greatest military leaders have retreated tactically to achieve their ultimate aim. One does not get into fights one is bound to lose. Only a useless general says that he can cut down trees with a finger. History gives us many examples. I need only mention Alexander the Great's patience when he finally managed to take Tyre from the Phoenicians in 332 BC. Indeed, it took even Alexander two, almost three, years and several peace treaties.'

The bishop was greeted with tepid applause.

Richard gazed out over the gathering. He saw mainly surprise in the faces before him, and relief.

No one spoke in opposition to Walter or Richard, but neither was there any enthusiasm on show. That same day

Richard appointed Hubert Walter as his closest counsellor. Richard gave him orders to remain in the Holy Land for a month after he himself had left.

On 9 October, Richard sailed from Acre. After an enforced stop for shelter at Corfu, they reached the Italian mainland at Aquileia. It would have been simplest to sail to the French coast but, because of a war between Toulouse and Berengaria's Navarre, it was impossible. The final leg had to be overland. Richard had four knights in his entourage. All were disguised as pilgrims in monks' habits. Richard had made a number of enemies among his Crusader allies during his stay in the Holy Land. Many of them had gone home and were seeking an opportunity for revenge. Richard thought it would lower the morale of the faithful if he, at the head of his own army, were to march home through Europe with unfinished business. After three weeks of travelling overland, they reached the town of Graz, which none of them knew, on 14 November.

He was barely acquainted with his companions. Their job was to get the king home unscathed. Richard wanted to be alone. He didn't want to share his shame. Only he could know the extent of his defeat. If he'd unburdened himself to anyone, he would have achieved nothing except forcing himself to watch the sorrow of his own misadventure reflected in the other's eyes and then have to explain the why and the how.

The five disguised knights sat round a fire on the outskirts of Graz. Richard asked if they knew what had happened to him at the battle of Ascalon.

They all shook their heads and looked at Richard. He felt relief.

'Well, tell us,' the men said.

'A soldier—a peasant, I think he was from Maine, I can't recall his name, a very brave man—and I managed to get away from Saladin's forces.'

'Just the two of you? With Saladin and his best soldiers close by?'

'We got away,' said Richard.

'Let no one say, Sire, that you're quick to blow your own trumpet.'

Richard got up and went to the nearest bushes to urinate. More than anything he wanted to retreat from the world, not because he had enemies but because he had friends.

20

On their first evening, just as dusk had fallen on the flowers, Richard managed to rent an attic room. As soon as they'd arrived in Graz they had decided, for reasons of security, to live separately and resume their journey in three days' time. Before Richard had spoken to the landlord, he had removed his gold ring with its three engraved lions and put it in his leather pouch. Only by convincing his landlord that he was a peaceable monk returning from the Holy Land was he able to rent a cheap room.

The room had a bed and a washing bowl on a stool. When he put his hands in the bowl, the water overflowed. He removed his hands and stared at the tiny movements in the water, which gradually stilled. He looked at his reflection. His cheekbones, nose and chin were picked out in the light from the window, shadow left the rest in darkness. He could just make out two eyes in the mirror's half-darkness. Could he see a trace of green in one? No, wasn't it mostly just black? His shoulders were visible. His pale skin highlighted a pair of powerful upper arms which stood out in strong contrast to the dark background. His pale brown freckles showed clearly. He shivered. His torso was bare and he was cold.

His monk's habit lay on the bed together with a small leather pouch containing a few coins and an olive sprig he'd taken from Gethsemane. The face in front of him might have belonged to a tailor, a squire or a highway robber.

Richard stared into his mirror. He saw a man, his beard unkempt, his red hair matted close to his head in places. The man was powerfully built. The hairs on his chest were sandy in colour. His mouth moved, its lips dry, the cheeks sun-scorched and not yet healed. The scar on his throat had got no prettier. His tongue and teeth were there. The man talked to the mirror.

He awoke refreshed the following day and went out. Leafless trees threw long shadows in the cold alleys. He roamed around peering at strangers' faces. All his life he'd been the one who'd been stared at. Perhaps as a child one looks at faces differently from an adult? But possibly as an adult one isn't so good at seeing the essence of a face? One has probably seen so many that it's become a habit, like getting dressed, eating, going to bed, getting up? But did he really wish to stare at anyone for a long time? No, that would be to form a tie. Was that the reason he'd been unable to form a bond with Berengaria? They could both have profited from sharing confidences. She had said they were like pawns in a game.

By the time evening came, he'd spoken to no one. He crept up to his room, fearful that his host should ask how his day had gone. Unobserved, he lay down on his bed, lonely, without armour, without a shell. If he'd had a dog, he thought, one he trusted, he would have trotted after it, and if the dog had begun to whine sorrowfully, he would have whined too. Was Wolf still alive?

Next day Richard decided to try to seek a friend, a person who needed to be no more than he was. How easy it was for such people. He stood for a long time in the alley where he lodged trying to decide which direction to take. A donkey and its driver sauntered past. Suddenly, and without provocation as far as Richard could see, the man began to beat the donkey on the back with a stick. Dust and flies rose into the air. Richard decided to go in the opposite direction.

Of all the people he'd met in adult life, very few were his real intimates, doubtless because only the rarest of them could think of him as anything but a king, and not just any king at that. Richard walked purposefully to one of the monastery's alehouses. Monks and pilgrims, who could speak several languages, were among its customers. It didn't take him long to get into conversation with a man on the subject of troubadour poetry, and the poet Walther von der Vogelweide in particular. But suddenly the man had to leave, just as Richard thought they were talking in the way ordinary people did. Richard suggested they could meet again in the same place that evening. Then he would pay for the mead, if the man didn't object. The man, whom Richard guessed was considerably older than himself, nodded. After they'd arranged the meeting and the man had disappeared, Richard walked about the town wondering if he would actually turn up. There really was something like closeness between them, wasn't there, when they talked about ghazals and end rhymes and von der Vogelweide?

The hour approached. It would be pleasant to continue their talk. Richard would insist on paying for the round. Not just because he'd promised but because he wanted to. The sun had begun its downward trajectory. He put his head round the door. The man wasn't there.

Richard was glad it was almost dark in the tap room. At least none of the other guests could see the disappointment in his eyes. He waited, ordered. The man didn't come. That was all. He didn't curse. He said nothing, he kept his words and his thoughts to himself. If it had been war he would have howled with rage. He sat on for a long time and had several drinks. He became more and more weighed down with mead. Perhaps someone would come and sit down and tell him a good anecdote or some tall story?

He gave up and tried to rise. He was pushed down again. He raised his head and looked straight into the eyes of his friend. He hadn't noticed that he had such a stoop. Richard couldn't leave now. Or could he? He stayed where he was. More drink was ordered. They talked for a long time, especially Richard.

'People don't believe in fate,' Richard said suddenly, 'except when there's no more to hope for. There's nothing so meagre.'

The other man began to talk about something Richard didn't understand before turning to an adjacent table. Richard went out and adjusted his habit. He liked wearing it. He wouldn't have minded his name dispersing into the wind or the water.

Richard got up, yawned the remains of the previous day out of his body. He looked down at his thirty-six-year-old body, his stomach and thighs were beginning to fill out. He talked aloud to himself. He argued, negotiated, beseeched and fervently prayed that God would forgive all his sins. Then he fell completely silent, as if listening to a voice within himself, before letting out a string of oaths and invective. It was as if he was liberating himself, knot by knot, from the naked certainty that lonely he was and lonely he would remain.

Hubert Walter should, following the plan they'd both made, have left the Holy Land. It wouldn't be long before he saw Eleanor, his beloved mother. It had been an age since they'd last seen one another. Was that why he couldn't recall a single one of her faults? He wondered if they didn't differ in one respect. She seemed to be more determined than he was. She made up her mind more quickly and acted on what she'd decided even more forcefully than he did.

What would he say to her? Was Hubert loyal to him and Eleanor? Before Richard went to the Holy Land he would never have asked himself such questions. He hated the uncertainty that grew in his head. One moment he wanted to vanish with the letters in his name. The next he told himself that he had a mother and subjects who were waiting for him and who needed him. Why should he blame himself for the defeat? The truth was that it was impossible to take Jerusalem with the army he'd had at his disposal. He had to return home to save what was possible to save. Philip had been playing havoc for more than a year. Had he conquered the whole of Normandy? And what had John been up to? Would he have got the support of some of his father's friends in the nobility and occupied part of England? An alliance between John and Philip would be the worst thing imaginable. England and the Angevin Kingdom, the western part of France, belonged to Richard and no one else. He was its king.

Eleanor and the people of those two great realms were waiting for him. He had failed them long enough. Just as Jerusalem had needed him to lead the army and take its capital back, so it was with his two beloved kingdoms. Now it was their turn. He stood up and looked out on Graz, which could have been any old town, apart from Jerusalem, the only city he hadn't managed to conquer. So far.

If only Saladin would cease haunting him, night after night. Perhaps he would have let him pray in the Church of the Holy Sepulchre, as others had been allowed to, and maybe the sultan wouldn't have killed him in an ambush afterwards. These things weren't impossible. You don't have dinner with your enemy, you kill him. Richard couldn't share the city with any one but those who followed the one true faith, his own. No compromise was possible. Not just one, but all the popes he knew of, believed the same as he did. One pope can be wrong but not all of them.

That same morning the five disguised knights rode northward. Richard rested his gaze on the habits of the two knights in front of him.

What is a human being?, he thought.

People lie down, night after night. They think, they remember, they fall to the ground like leaves. People turn in the dark. The world surrounds them. The skull envelops the thoughts. The clothes cover the body. The body encases the bones, the skin the flesh, the wind shrouds the night, the sand covers the desert.

What is a human being? A fable without words.

Do you dream as you die—do you find a new language the living cannot hear?

Richard glanced up at the sky. The clouds were pushing northwards.

It was cold. He was wondering if there would be rain or sleet when he was struck by a blow on the back of the head.

II
DÜRNSTEIN

The narrow track was bordered by a prickly pear or two. Further ahead, four men dressed in long white robes were walking. Two donkeys trudged after them, loaded with baskets full of clay and stones. The last of the sun's rays gilded the mountaintops. In the west the sky held a lingering trace of red, pink and green. Behind the sandblasted rocks, not unlike fallen clouds, the darkness unfolded from the depths of the horizon. The darkness and the wind erased the marks of the hyena's tracks on the dune. The noise of the dromedary greedily chewing the wild rose ceased. Silence would reign until the sun arose once more and began its climb to the zenith, like a newly born eye.

1

The snow on the mountaintops was dirty. At their foot lay rocks, large and small, which had released their grip. A golden eagle trimmed its right wing to swoop to the left above the juniper bushes, heather and a couple of withered, pink rhododendrons.

Pines stalked the treeline. An ibex rubbed it horns against a fallen trunk. Down the valley stood larch, lime and maple. The leaves that still clung to the trees were yellow and brown.

In the valley bottom, between the high wooded mountainsides, ran a wide, meandering river like an artery in the landscape. On its bank lay a small village with a main street, a square and a white church. The sky above the houses and the church spire, where, a few years earlier, projectiles had arced and the smoke from burning witches had risen, was quiet. Directly above the village, on a shelf of rock, lay the palace and fortress of Dürnstein.

Richard knelt in the cold, yellow grass. His hands were tied behind his back. His ring with its three lions had gone. He stared at his guards. They wore yellow and blue uniforms striped with red. They kicked him and laughed. Richard screamed. A kick to his right side made him topple forwards. He gasped and moaned. This made them kick him several more times before gagging him.

'You've been given clear instructions not to harm him,' said a voice in front of him, which he took to be the commander's.

'Why must he be blindfolded?' asked someone else.

Richard received a blow and lost consciousness.

The chill brought him round. He was lying on his stomach. He raised his head from the floor and tried to lift the arms that were tied behind him before he made an attempt to stand.

He fell forwards and lay still until he tried again to wriggle round. He laid his cheek to the floor. It felt like hard-tramped earth. He rubbed his face against it to loosen his blindfold, but to no avail. Wasn't there a little warmth emanating from one corner? He tried to creep closer to its source. It must be a torch.

After much effort Richard managed to get to his knees.

Where had he been when they were attacked? How many of them were there? Surely he must be able to remember some of it? Were they in the vicinity of a river? How had he got here? Were they highway robbers? No, they had uniforms.

Here was the King of England, the hope of mankind, the pope's favourite and God's greatest weapon, stuck in semi-darkness, in a damp, dank dungeon, gagged and blindfolded.

2

'Let me out! Who are you?' he shouted.

He pushed himself forwards so that his head was closer to the sounds outside the door. Didn't they realize what would happen once the abduction was discovered by his powerful allies? The punishment would be worse than anything they could imagine. He wouldn't tell them anything. If he did, they would demand a ransom. Or kill him.

Eleanor, Berengaria, Hubert Walter and his people would never put up with this indignity. They would be furious.

Richard managed to sit upright, and shuddered. How would Philip celebrate when he heard the news that he was taken prisoner? And John—would he proclaim himself King of England as quickly as possible?

He rebuked himself for having realized far too late that John was obsessed with being regent. The puppy had no ideals. Like a dog, he would run after the nearest bone.

Eventually he managed to get to his feet without falling and went on a little round of his cell before he began jumping up and down to keep warm. Could Philip, John and Tancred of Sicily be in league? Were they the ones behind this? It was possible, wasn't it?

No, but of course—why hadn't he thought of it?—it was the sultan. It was Saladin, helped by his brother. It was quite possible they'd followed him and struck when his party had least expected it. They could have joined forces with one of his many enemies. Perhaps this was the start of an attack on Europe?

'Saladin!' he shouted.

Of course it could be Saladin.

He felt the heat of a flame. Was it a torch? He moved closer to it but stopped abruptly, frightened of burning himself.

'Lord, reveal yourself to my mother and show her, as only you can, that I'm alive. She is one of your most obedient servants. But promise me . . . *please*,' he corrected himself, 'make sure she doesn't learn that I've negotiated with the Antichrist.'

Help would come, of course. It would take a few days, perhaps a couple of weeks. But no longer. The pope, God indeed, would have to get him out of here. Was anyone better able to lead a new Crusade than him? But what if they'd heard of his treachery? After all, he was the one who'd given the order to retreat.

How long had he been here in the dungeon? He would have liked to read, yet again, *Li Romanz del Chevalier au Lion*, the story about the knight Yvain at the court of King Arthur where all the king's men gathered. Richard recalled the plot in detail—Yvain wanted to avenge his cousin and vanquish the unknown person who had

murdered him. Yvain killed the man but fell in love with
Laudine, his widow. Yvain and Laudine married. As soon
as the wedding was over, Yvain went off to a joust. He forgot to return home at the appointed time. She refused to
see him again. Yvain was prostrate with grief. But in the
end he was reconciled with his beloved Laudine. Richard
went through the story out loud.

Why had this entered his head now? Because he was
as desolate as Yvain had been? But Yvain had someone he
really loved. Of course Berengaria was beautiful, she was
from the Spanish aristocracy and well educated but to love
her as Yvain had loved his Laudine? It was impossible. No,
he'd long realized that the great Roman poet Ovid had
been right—to love your wife is impossible. He wasn't
aware of a single example to the contrary in his circle of
acquaintance, apart from Philip and Isabel. But he and
Yvain shared certain similarities— like Yvain he was the
most famous knight in the world. And didn't Yvain's longing to be reunited with Laudine bear a strong resemblance
to his high regard for the lovely city of Jerusalem?

Richard hadn't heard noises or sounds from anyone
apart from his gaolers. Surely the people at home must
work out where he was imprisoned soon? What had happened to the other knights he'd been travelling with? Had
they managed to get away?

A bat was fluttering in his breast. Richard banged his
head against the stone wall. Blood pumped around his
head, the ancient blood, the blood he'd had no part in
choosing, which was part of his line, which had been
bequeathed to him, and which had been circulating for so
long before it came down to him.

3

The door was pushed open with great effort. It was clearly heavy. Its hinges creaked. Richard turned in the direction of the sound. He heard a man approaching him with purposeful step.

'Prisoner, in my left hand I'm holding a piece of cloth. It's tattered and filthy.'

The voice sounded disguised. The man was speaking French but it was hardly his native language.

'It was once a beautiful standard. Fastened to the red background are three golden lions, one above the other.'

'Who are you?'

There was no answer. Why didn't he reply? Was the stranger standing there studying him?

Richard tried to rise but fell over on to his side. He could hear that the man was drawing a sword from a scabbard. Richard flinched as he felt something sharp rasp his cheek. With a quick movement he tried to twist himself away.

'You resemble a worm that has lain too long under a stone. I think you've got paler during the three months you've been here.'

The man laughed.

Several others entered the room.

'One of my soldiers has a bowl of soup, the other a mug of beer. And just to be friendly, I've put out writing materials that you may need at some time.'

Richard heard the soldiers placing the objects on the floor and sprinting out again. In a moment they were back. The scraping noises on the floor caused him to think they'd fetched chairs and tables.

'The soup is a speciality of the region. It's made from lamb. There are some pieces of meat in it.'

'Can you loosen the rope round my arms and take my blindfold off?'

The man led Richard to the chair.

'Don't worry. I'll help you eat. Have you heard anything from your mother recently?'

Richard didn't answer.

He felt the heat of what was being raised to his mouth and hesitated a second before he opened his jaws.

'Perhaps Queen Eleanor was the last person to feed you like this but then, I suppose it was usually the servants who did it?'

There was definitely something familiar about the voice. Richard choked on some soup and began to cough.

'That almost went down the wrong way,' said the stranger. 'Let's try one more time. Can you tell me your name?'

'George.'

Richard was scalded. He cried out. He cried out for all the times he'd burnt himself.

'Did you taste the flavour of the meat? The sheep were grazed in the mountains.'

Richard was lifted out of the chair and laid on what he thought must have been a thin blanket.

'How long is it since you saw your mother? You wish her well, don't you? I've just spoken to her. She was surprised you'd been taken prisoner.'

'You're bluffing.'

The man kicked Richard's legs. Richard groaned.

'Did you recognize it?'

'What do you mean?'

'The boot, I was wearing it the last time we met. They're my favourite pair. I really hope you'll see them quite soon.'

Who was this idiot who thought he could scare him with such talk?

'They're very smart,' the man went on. 'Brown pigskin, pointed toes and they reach three inches above the ankles. It wouldn't take an expert to tell they were expensive. They're laced, the skin is shiny and impregnated with fat.'

'They sound like serpents' tongues.'

The material under Richard was snatched away.

'D'you know what I'm holding in front of your face, that you've just been lying on? It's your standard from the time you were in the Holy Land.'

Richard tried to listen to the voice with particular care but he still couldn't work out who it belonged to.

'Where did you steal it?'

'I bought it from one of your knights.'

Richard was lifted on to a chair. The standard was stuffed into his mouth with considerable force. He turned his head from side to side gasping for air.

The banner was yanked out. He felt a flat-handed blow to his back.

It knocked all the wind out of him. His body swayed to and fro. He was about to fall out of his chair but was pulled back up again. After a while his breath returned. He felt somebody shaking him.

'Still alive?'

Richard noted the anxiety in the voice before him.

'You're bluffing.'

'Guards! Fetch what's lying on the bench outside the dungeon door!'

Something soft, with an indefinable smell, was pushed into Richard's face.

'Smell it. She gave it to me. A pillow she's saved for thirty years. Your first pillow. She gave it to me so that you'd know I really had met her. You must have a good relationship.'

Did it smell of sour milk, or puke? Richard wasn't sure.

'I must see it before I believe you.'

'I remember your father's funeral. I was there, in the church at Fontevrault. You must have loved him dearly.'

The man paced slowly round him.

'When you stared into the open coffin.'

'Be quiet,' Richard exclaimed.

'You stared at his body for a long time before you hurried out.'

Richard sat quite still.

'You have a tendency to flee when things get too much, when armour and mail are useless? You won't get away now.'

'Father is a skeleton,' Richard said, and clenched his teeth. 'Your speaking to my mother is nothing but a lie.'

'We have no reason to harm your mother. You'll soon see why. She's fine, lives and eats well, and isn't blindfolded.'

'Don't pretend she's your prisoner too.'

'Remember what Abbot Joakim of Fiore in Calabria, the pope's closest supporter, himself said?'

The man reeled off the words fluently. His voice was derisive, rasping, he hid his accent well. For a moment Richard thought it was Frederik I Barbarossa's son, Henry VI. But this voice was deeper. Surely, it couldn't be . . . Richard felt the stirrings of something reminiscent of fear.

'You remember how the abbot said that mankind had passed through several phases and that the final one would be ushered in by us in the Third Crusade? We were the chosen who would conquer the unbelievers in the Holy Land. He also said that Saladin was the Devil's ultimate representative on earth.'

'Please.'

'You, Richard the Lionheart, you, and not I, were selected by the abbot, on behalf of the pope, God's representative on Earth, to be the foremost Crusader, Christendom's finest warrior, the bravest and most valorous of us all.'

'Be quiet,' Richard shouted and tried to stand.

'You were the one who was to kill the Devil's dagger, Sultan Saladin. You bragged about what you'd learnt from General Rodrigo del Bivar-el Cid about beating Saladin's fast cavalry.'

'It's *you* . . . Leopold! What have you done with my mother?'

'We're negotiating with her. When I gave her your beautiful gold ring, she realized I was serious.'

'Serious?'

'I'm not prepared to discuss your mother before you've listened to my story without interrupting me. I want to see your eyes while I'm speaking.'

Duke Leopold tore the blindfold from Richard's face.

4

'There are many things we forget in life. Most things, presumably. But certain events we remember better than others, right down to the smallest detail. You were mounted on your white horse, Richard, in the midst of us knights. The walls of Acre towered in the distance. The evening sun was low and red. Saladin had managed to hold the city. We sat there in our heavy armour, helmets in our hands, hair and beards damp with sweat.'

Richard looked straight into the light blue eyes. The lips beneath were twitching.

'Guy de Lusignan, king of Jerusalem, was staring straight at you. That numskull was staring at you with admiration. Every time I made a suggestion, you cut me off. Remember how I suggested we should attack the nearest ridge to sever Saladin's supply line? It wouldn't have taken more than a couple of hundred men. You shook your head.'

'I'm not . . .'

'You thought we'd have a better chance of beating Saladin in a bigger battle on the plain. The men glanced at you before looking at each other. You all began to sneer. My soldiers were formed up close by. You asked me to accompany you out of the circle. You were in charge. I went with you. We rode towards my men. When we got to my own standard-bearer you stopped your horse, grabbed the standard and told my household troops to tie up ten of my men and chase the remainder back to the main force. They obeyed you! You might as well have assaulted me. You raised our banner and looked at it, hurled it into the dust, got off your horse and trampled on it.'

'Believe me, I don't remember anything,' Richard said.

He could hear the submissiveness in his own voice. He wasn't afraid of death, but this man wouldn't relinquish him without the worst of torments.

'The pope needed you as a hero. You kicked me out of the Holy Land.'

'You fled!' Richard shouted.

Leopold cuffed him.

'After you humiliated me in front of my own soldiers. You called me an incompetent fool! Remember how Guy laughed, out of pure fear, fear of not winning your approval! That was how scared he was of being left isolated, like me.'

'What is it you've been negotiating with my mother?'

'Your head. Henry, the Holy Roman emperor and my overlord in Regensburg, has asked me to begin an auction between the pope, Philip, John and Saladin—is there anyone I've forgotten? Ah yes, your mother, and Hubert Walter. No offers have been received as yet.'

Leopold drew breath and said, derision in his voice, 'It's a poor show, isn't it, when your mother won't make an offer for her own son, the king, her darling?'

'I'm proud of her. She won't have anything to do with blackguards like you. I'll be freed before long. Are the pair of you in league with Philip?'

Leopold turned on his heel and left him.

Richard could see out through a crack in the stone wall. There were some spruce trees outside.

How could God allow the emperor and Leopold to insult him in this way? What had those two done for believers? He had led the Crusaders and fought a Saracen general no one had prepared him for. Not even God. Why had God allowed him to be taken prisoner by this rogue who had only one thought: To make money out of him? Perhaps God wished to be alone, as he had been before he created the world and mankind? Was that why he allowed even Christians to kill one another? Why didn't the pope assemble an army to free him instead of entering into negotiations with these knaves? Wasn't Hubert Walter at home by now? What made Leopold think that the pope, his mother and Walter would make offers? If he ever got home, he would beat John and Philip cruelly and decisively. They would all find out that he was still the great warrior.

Exhausted, Richard seated himself at the table and thought of Sisyphus' tireless toil in rolling the stone to the top of the hill. The first time his mother had told him the Greek myth, he'd been fascinated by the patience of Sisyphus. His mother had regarded Richard with soft eyes, the eyes he'd never known waver before anyone. The earnestness in her voice and the detailed and vivid description of the dusty, stony upland made him smell the dust and feel the sharp pain of stones beneath his feet. He had never forgotten Eleanor's words that the very struggle to get the stone to the summit was enough to fill a human heart. Should he feel satisfied with himself because he'd *tried* to conquer Jerusalem? If he hadn't had a large enough army, or he lacked weapons, or had been beset by a storm—no, a fissure that had opened up in the earth—it might be arguable. But he had no such excuse. And both God and his mother knew it.

Would she forgive him for not reaching his goal? Never. And the pope, the cardinals; think of Lefevre, who had translated and enunciated Pope Gregory VIII's bull, which had made him take the Cross. And what of all the bishops, priests, kings and knights who—in common with all believers, high and low—had depended on him? Would they ever feel confidence in him again? Why should his mother or anyone else pay a ransom for him? The fact that he hadn't yet been freed was a sign that she and Hubert Walter no longer trusted him.

He began to think of some of his old horses. When they were no longer up to the job he couldn't bear to slaughter them, but lightened their burdens as much as possible. He took off bags and harness. But they, in their wisdom, realized after a while that the time had come. They left the herd and disappeared.

Did his mother want him to do the same?

5

Richard jumped up and down in front of the torch to keep warm. It felt as if the cold was eating into his joints and marrow of his bones.

Did Hildegard of Bingen recommend anything against the cold? He couldn't recall reading about it. The first time he'd come across the nun's works was at the court in Poitou; its mixture of wisdom, beauty, experience and pointed comment had enthralled him from the first. She wasn't merely an abbess, she was the 'Sibyl of the Rhine', a philosopher and composer, she was also the finest of apothecaries. 'Disease is a sign from God,' she had written.

'Then disease brings Heaven closer to Earth, doesn't it?' Richard mumbled.

If Hildegard had been a man, she would have been clad in a suit of armour, lifted on to a horse and handed a lance. He was sure of it. It was God who had preordained her life, just as he had Richard's. Both were learned and brave, with a developed sense of beauty. Richard had heard Hildegard's songs accompanied by harp, organ and flute at the castle at Poitou, exactly as they'd been performed in her convent at Eibingen. Music, only good music of course, was itself an expression of the longing for proximity with the divine, she believed. Richard agreed.

He stood on tiptoe, remained there for a moment before lowering his heels. He repeated the movement several times. Took a pace forwards and stood by the wall. He lifted his face and felt the heat from the torch above him. It was too high up to burn him. A gentle warmth just managed to reach his brow and the bridge of his nose but wasn't strong enough to penetrate his body.

He tried to imagine his mother's library and its three volumes by Hildegard the nun.

He opened his mouth and tried to breathe in as much heat as possible from the air above him.

'Hildegard, you who said that you were a piece of down buoyed up by God's breath, I need your advice. I need the strength of the spruce to be able to get through this, don't I?'

Why did God allow Saladin to prevent him from taking Jerusalem? Because the Lord had a plan, didn't he? Couldn't God tell him that Saladin was a charlatan, an evil creature—assure him and his mother that they hadn't been wrong? Saladin said that he forgave, that he wouldn't avenge himself later. Richard turned his head to the floor and let his forehead rest against the cold stone wall.

Saladin possessed a strength that came from within, from without . . . from everywhere. When Richard spoke his name, his strength ran from his shoulders, through his upper arms and forearms, into his hands and out through his fingers.

Al-Adil had called him Lionheart.

'Lion,' mumbled Richard, and thought of strength, constancy, loyalty and pride. The lion could stare into the sun without narrowing its eyes, according to the *Bestiar-ium*, in which he'd read about the true and imagined characteristics of real or mythological creatures. He enjoyed reading about how animals' traits affected their virtues and vices. But, he realized suddenly, the lion could also be evil. And violence, cynicism, fury and the ability to engender fear were the hallmarks of Satan. When al-Adil had reported on their meetings to his brother, he must have laughed and scoffed at the conceited Crusader king. How many of the lion's qualities did he really possess? Certainly not the lion's ability to wipe out its tracks with its tail.

The problem was greater because everything he did was noticed, even when he tried to shroud himself in a monk's habit. But which lion was he made of more—the good or the evil? Before he arrived at Acre he would have been sure that it was the good. Those unsettled glances he'd received from the knights around him after the executions, planted a suspicion that he also had some of the evil lion in him. It must be captivity that was confusing him!

Leopold opened the heavy door.

'I have good news, Richard. Last evening, Emperor Henry feted me with a banquet in Vienna in honour of the Crusaders' victory over Saladin's forces at Acre. After the battle my tunic was so saturated with blood that when I took it off, it was only white where the belt had pinched. Emperor Henry has therefore decreed that I'm to have the colours red and white in my standard. With white in the middle. Just imagine—he bowed deeply as he presented it to me.'

Richard looked at his nostrils. They were flaring, his eyes were turning watery. The puffed up peacock was moved to tears. What a nincompoop. Leopold gabbled away, as some people do, because they think God won't have the heart to let them die half way through a sentence.

'What is a human being after all?' Leopold asked suddenly looking straight at Richard. Without waiting for an answer, he went on: 'He's a talking, two-legged creature who spends his life seeking the longest route to the grave.'

Richard couldn't be bothered to listen to any more of this self-important prattle.

He dropped down on all fours. The duke crossed to him in three heavy strides to pull him up.

'What are you doing?' Richard shouted, waving him away. 'Don't kill him. Shoo!'

He stared at the floor as if pretending to study some invisible insect.

'What are you playing at?' Leopold asked uneasily.

'Go away, stand over by the wall, Leopold, before you do something seriously wrong,' Richard said emphatically, and whispered in the direction of the floor: 'Come to Daddy.'

'You're telling me where I'm to stand now? Have you completely lost your wits?'

'You've always been a bumbler, Leopold. Don't move! You're killing him. He doesn't know you.'

'I didn't think things were as bad as this . . . Can't you wait till the ransom arrives before going mad?'

'D'you know what he's called? Little Saladin.' Richard smiled down at the floor. 'Get him!'

Richard laughed.

It was good to see the uncertainty spread across Leopold's face, Richard thought, as the duke slammed the door behind him.

Richard got up and began walking in a circle. Were they all in a conspiracy against him—Eleanor, Hubert Walter, John, Emperor Henry, Leopold and the pope? Didn't they realize that the only winner in all this was Saladin?

Where did such thoughts come from? He wasn't really going mad, was he? Certainly it was principled of his mother not to pay Leopold a single mark, but if it wasn't followed up quickly with a force to set him free, it meant that she'd surrendered him.

6

Richard heard singing outside. It must be a troubadour. He could hear that the song was in German but he couldn't make out the words. Should he call out? What if it were his old friend, Blondel, out there. Was there anyone who sang more beautifully?

The voice was a little deeper than Blondel's, and pleasant to listen to. Surely it couldn't be the one he'd heard so much about, the most famous of the German-speaking troubadours? Could it be Walther von der Vogelweide? The poet who always travelled with a lute on his back. He'd been a popular, if very poor, troubadour, until Bishop Wolfger von Passau gave him a more regular income. As a rule Walther earned his money at Leopold's court in Babenberg, where the appearance of a skilled poet as a visitor was always popular. He'd learnt his art from Reinmar the Elder, the master he always acknowledged when asked how he'd become so proficient. There, outside Richard's cell, the troubadour sang. Why shouldn't it be Walther, standing out there performing one of his most famous songs? Richard searched his mind for a moment before remembering one of his verses:

> Beneath a lime tree
> On a moor

Where lately we two lay
The wind caressingly
Rocked our bower
Of harvest flowers and hay
Before the greenwood in a vale
Tandaradei!
Sang so pure a nightingale.

Could that be what he was hearing?

The air was warm, Richard could feel it even where he was. He stood on tiptoe. He saw the lute resting against a post. The man he took to be the troubadour alternated between sitting and lying in the meadow outside. By his side lay a girl of barely eighteen. They seemed certain that no one could see them, and it looked as if Walther was filled with only one desire—to seduce the girl who lay on the large, thick woollen rug listening to the young but already famous poet. He would doubtless be telling her that he'd made his will and that in it he'd left all his worldly goods to the monastery at Würzburg, provided the monks put out bread for the birds each day on his grave. Poets are poets. And did she sigh, Richard wondered, before asking what he owned, to which the poet gave a vague answer?

The whole meadow was green. Here and there grew what looked like herd's grass and the occasional bluebell. The sun had just passed its zenith when Walther rose and raised his lute so that his fingers could touch the strings.

Richard shouted as loudly as he could.

Richard listened carefully as the lute's introductory notes came through the air.

He shouted again.

The singer stopped. Both he and the girl ran in the direction of the sound.

'I am King Richard of England!'

He saw them clearly. A couple of guards came up and chased them away.

That afternoon Richard took up the writing materials Leopold had given him. For eight months they'd lain untouched on the bench in the corner. Richard wrote:

> *No man who's jailed can tell his purpose well*
> *adroitly, as if he could feel no pain;*
> *but to console him, he can write a song.*
> *I've many friends, but all their gifts are poor;*
> *they'd be ashamed to know for ransom now*
> *two winters I've been jailed.*

They didn't see me, thought Richard, but they must have heard me. From that moment on rumours began to circulate, in Austria and then in other dukedoms, countries and countships, that he'd been taken prisoner and was possibly still alive.

7

The sunbeams slanted down from the hole high in the wall. Richard tried to force his eyes to pick out a single ray. It was at once sharp and colourless. It revealed every detail on the floor—a fly, a splinter, a piece of fluff he hadn't seen before. Now all of it was visible. He even managed to discover an ant on the edge of the light. The ant wanted its share of the heat. He'd stripped to the waist and lay on the floor, dawdling where the sunbeams were warmest.

Richard was carrying his mother through the streets and alleys of Jerusalem. He held her in his arms while crowds, apostles, priests, cardinals, bishops, archangels and the pope cheered him. And there, right at the back, was a tall man, with long hair and beard. The whole of the city smelt of incense. Richard coughed.

The commandant opened the door and woke him. He was handcuffed and led out, across the passage and to the outside door. Nothing was said. When the door opened, he was dazzled. He turned his back to the sun.

'I'm so pleased to see you, Richard. I ordered my men to remove the standard so that you wouldn't be tempted to hang yourself.'

Duke Leopold sat in the castle grounds, eating alone. Quails' eggs, duck fillets, carp and fruits of all colours lay on the table in front of him. He described the view to Richard. The village and the Danube to the west, in the opposite direction they could see Tulln on the other side of the promontory. The mountains on either side of the wide, calm, slow-flowing river stretched tall and jagged southwards, towards the Tirol and Kärnten. Richard's gaze was caught by a buzzard.

'I thought you might enjoy a little sun,' said the duke. 'You see the wagtail, the way it flicks its tail? And there, on top of the castle roof . . . can you make out the swallows? They're flying high today.'

'What is it you want?' Richard broke in.

'The time has come,' said Leopold, and drew his long sword from its scabbard.

Richard turned towards the two soldiers on guard. Their crossbows were pointing at him.

'Shoot!'

Richard just managed to glimpse the projectiles leaving the strings. He closed his eyes.

The bolts just missed and buried themselves in a wooden partition behind him.

'You've seen that weapon before. I offered you two hundred of them as we sat on horseback outside the walls of Acre. "They can't even bring down an unarmed man," was your answer.'

Richard turned his eyes to the red-and-white flag that flew straight from the highest tower.

'We've received an offer.'

Leopold gave Richard a sidelong glance. Richard pretended not to have heard.

'We've been offered twenty thousand marks and for Sicily to become part of the Holy Roman Empire. Do you want to know who made the offer?'

Richard shrugged his shoulders.

'Do you know what answer we gave?'

'It wasn't my mother at any rate.'

'No, it wasn't her. She's forgotten you. Did you know that the Holy Roman emperor and the pope met in Rome a few days ago?'

'What had the pope to say?' Richard asked.

'His Holiness requested me to put some questions to you before helping you to the next life. The pope believes that answering honestly will make a difference to your destination, whether it's eternal torment or salvation. I advise you, Richard, to be honest. The quicker you admit that you've been in league with Saladin, the better it will be.'

'In league?'

'Do you deny that you were in contact with his family?'

'I don't know what you mean.'

'Several of my men and other knights have seen you with Saladin's brother.'

'On one occasion,' Richard replied.

'If you can lie about that, you can lie about anything. I must remind you that I'm enquiring on behalf of His Holiness the Pope, no less. What really happened after the battle at Acre, Richard? Did you really meet Saladin's brother a few days afterwards?'

'Don't you think I was tough enough on the Saracens? Why do you want me to repeat something you already know—that we captured thousands of soldiers, women and children, and that I killed many of them with my own hands while Saladin watched?'

'I know that you talked to Saladin's brother right after the battle of Acre.'

'No.'

'Surely you remember his name?'

'No.'

'Does the name "al-Adil" mean anything to you'

'Yes, that was it. I asked him about Saladin's health. I enjoyed hearing about the frail, malaria-ridden body and the mournful look on his face.'

'Why were you so concerned about how things stood with the infidels' leader?'

'For one reason. I wanted to get to know his weak points. Only that.'

'You're a traitor.'

'All my life I've wanted to perform one great deed. Taking Jerusalem from the Antichrist was the triumph I wanted, more than any other.'

'My cousin, Conrad of Montferrat, defeated Saladin at Tyre. Have you forgotten that? He was gathering all of us Crusaders. You were responsible for his murder. Admit it! Your people said it was the Assassins, but you arranged it, didn't you? You were envious and vengeful.'

'That's mad, it was the Assassins' suicide soldiers that killed him.'

'You deserve to die just for what you did to Conrad. This brother of Saladin, whose name you said you didn't know only a moment ago, gave you gifts. Don't you remember?'

'You haven't any proof.'

'It happened on at least four occasions. Don't you know that God can see you, Richard? The consideration Saladin showed you was a gesture to a fallen enemy. It was a noble deed with no risk attached.'

Richard admitted to himself that Leopold's words stung.

'Each time al-Adil came to meet me when I was ill, he brought doctors. They wanted to help me,' Richard said, surprised at how much he'd given away.

'Saladin has bewitched you.'

'He sent me poems.'

'How can you sell yourself to a Saracen because he sends you poems? The Devil can never create anything beautiful, neither can he show kindness. The pope will be interested to hear that you chose to view him in such a generous light.'

'There's been no one, believe me, absolutely no one—my father, my brother John, King Philip, the pope and Emperor Henry included—that I've hated more intensely than the sultan.'

Richard looked past the duke as if he was he were in his own world, before he turned his eyes on Leopold again.

'I've never hated you in the same way. You're too pathetic for that, too insignificant.'

Richard squinted up at the hole in the wall. An angry flash of lightning lit up his cell. A clap of thunder sounded before the rain began. The lightning continued and struck a nearby tree. He could hear it burning. Soon he caught the smell of scorched pine needles. People were shouting and hallooing outside. They must be the duke's soldiers. He could hear them dousing the fire. Was lightning the angry glance of God? Richard trembled.

Richard called the guards. He told them he had to speak to Leopold. The duke was with him shortly.

'I have a last request. I need birch as soon as possible. I feel that the last of my strength is about to ebb away.'

Anxiety waxed in Leopold's eyes. Richard spoke in lyrical terms about that bright tree, that modest tree, the tree of spring, the best fuel, the finest medicine for everything from scurvy and hair loss to rheumatism and boils. Could he, as it was nearing mid-summer, get some boiled birch leaves and buds? And, as the moon was waning, could the duke's helpers provide the buds that same evening?

Leopold nodded energetically. Richard was certain that it was the fear that his prisoner might die that made the duke's cheeks flame red.

'I'll get one of my people to make contact with the prioress of the convent in Eibingen, too. They're supposed to be very good at this sort of thing,' Leopold said.

The nun with the greatest knowledge of herbs at Eibingen had manufactured a healing ointment. Richard hoped she might prove as skilful as Hildegard of Bingen. But then, what was the point? If he'd died in the fight for

Jerusalem, at least his memory would be sacred and his mother would have been proud of him, he thought.

Most of the royal and noble houses were certain that Richard was in the Holy Land and that he went to High Mass at the Church of the Holy Sepulchre each Sunday. The rumours that he was held prisoner somewhere in Central Europe were trusted by very few. During High Mass in Wales, Navarre, Burgundy and Pisa, the bishops and priests gave thanks that Richard had, with his own hands, killed the Saracen sultan. The pope didn't disabuse them about Richard's victory but encouraged everyone to support the Templars and the Knights of the Order of St John and take the Cross to ensure victory. But the response was flagging. These stay-at-home monarchs claimed that their substance had been exhausted in the earlier Crusades.

8

Richard looked down at his chest and stomach. On the left side of his torso, beneath his heart, a scar shone out at him, a scar he'd never noticed before. As he stared, he saw more and more scars, and out of each scar grew feathers. The scars spread on to his arms and legs. His toes and fingers became curved claws. Soon he was covered in white down. The wind rose. Richard took off.

He flew through the narrow opening in his cell, out of the castle, across mountains and seas, to the Mount of Olives. He landed beneath an olive tree and looked out over Jerusalem in the searing afternoon light. A fresh gust of wind carried him on to places he only knew by name. He circled once over Golgotha. The crosses were still there. Richard glided low above the Via Dolorosa and followed Jesus on his way, bleeding as he went, carrying the Cross. Right behind Jesus was Saladin. How narrow and tortuous the Via Dolorosa was. He landed on the altar of the Church of the Holy Sepulchre, between two large silver candelabra. It was certainly no cathedral, it was one of the smallest churches he'd ever seen. He felt his feathers catch fire.

'Wake up!'

Richard rubbed the sleep out of his eyes and got to his knees.

'Emperor Henry owns your head,' said Leopold. 'He's decided you can keep it for one hundred and fifty thousand marks.'

Richard shrugged his shoulders.

A fly entered the cell and flew in its strange pattern. Richard let the fly settle on his chest, caught it at the first attempt. 'I know them. They fly backwards a bit before flying forwards.'

Richard held it in his hand, went to the small opening in the wall and released it.

'Leopold, no one can pay a sum equivalent to three English budgets.'

'I've come to take you to the emperor.'

'I don't understand.'

'The pope has indicted you for the murder of Conrad of Montferrat. The proceedings will be held in the emperor's castle.'

'It's madness to think I would have killed your cousin. He was one of the Crusaders I had most faith in.'

'I have another piece of news.'

'I'm not interested.'

'There's been an offer to pay the stated amount.'

'Liar.'

'The bidder has one condition. That you answer two questions.'

Richard nodded.

'Do you agree that Saladin isn't a believer?'

'Yes.'

'Would you have been able to kill Saladin?'

Richard didn't know what to say.

'Answer!'

Richard straightened his clothes. Leopold folded his arms and looked him in the eye.

'Saladin died on the third of March in Damascus. Aren't you pleased that the fool is dead?'

'Was he murdered? Or did he fall in battle?'

'From what I've heard he died of disease. Don't you find it galling that you didn't manage to kill him?'

Leopold scoffed.

Richard was bewildered at not being able to answer Leopold's question. Even worse was his lack of pleasure at hearing the tidings of this death.

'Who has raised such an inordinate sum?' Richard asked.

'You do have some interest, then?'

'I'd like to know who is stupid enough.'

'You have a self-sacrificing mother, Richard. It's possible that she'll see you alive again.'

'So your greed is greater than your desire to kill me?'

'Why should one preclude the other? First we'll get the money, after that we'll see what happens.'

'Was it God or the Devil who caused me to be seized?'

'D'you know the difference? My men kept you under observation from the ninth of October last year, when you sailed from Acre. We lost track of you but heard you'd been recognized crossing the Alps. You were with four men, weren't you—knights disguised as monks? It must have been a strenuous journey . . . We had you under our thumb right across Styria and all the way to Graz. Do you remember the elderly man you met a couple of times in the alehouse? He helped us when we thought you'd vanished.'

'What happened to the four others?'

'They weren't permitted to live.'

Leopold turned and shouted: 'Soldiers, make ready the carriage and take him to the emperor in Regensburg!'

Richard stroked his hair and beard. Could he be certain Leopold was telling the truth? If it were the case, why had Eleanor agreed to give them the money? It couldn't be her. Who else could have raised such a sum? The Church in England and the Angevin Kingdom? But they had spent most of what they possessed on the Crusade he'd led. If he got out, Leopold and Henry would repay it many times over.

Could King John have taken England, and Philip Anjou? Had John burnt down the towns he'd taken? As a boy John used to say a conqueror always ought to do that. Richard took a last look at the cell's earth floor, its walls and ceiling. He would have given a lot to witness the terrified eyes of John and Philip when, and if, he ever got out. The thought gave him something he hoped was strength.

The soldiers returned to fetch him. Leopold grasped Richard's shoulder. He shook the hand off.

'There is one man who has gained more than any other by my imprisonment,' Richard said. 'I'm not thinking of John, he's too weak. It must be Philip. You and Emperor Henry need an alliance with him to strengthen your relations with the pope. Philip would also give you better contact with Venice. Wouldn't he?'

Leopold shoved him towards the door: 'The carriage is waiting.'

9

As they emerged into the courtyard, Richard looked for opportunities to escape. He quickly realized it was impossible.

Inside the carriage sat two guards and a nun, who said her name was Anne Hofer and that she came from the convent at Eibingen. Fifty soldiers rode in front of the carriage and after it came Leopold and the commander with just over a hundred more. The dark-haired nun had brought with her the infusion of birch Richard had asked for. She told him she also had ash for rheumatic pains in her luggage. And dill to ease digestion and fennel against influenza and pneumonia. The nun was well dressed. Richard apologized that he wasn't in his usual raiment and asked why she looked so elegant. Like Hildegard of Bingen, Anne thought that dressing well was an important way of praising beauty, and God.

The Eibingen convent grew fennel as a vegetable, as a seasoning and for medicinal purposes. Anne believed that snakes ate fennel to sharpen their vision. She had also brought spruce and rose with her. Rose because Leopold had told her that the prisoner was irascible and quick-tempered.

Along with French, she could speak and write Latin. Richard noticed that the dress she wore was expensive.

Each time she seemed anxious, she would quickly pass her hand over her smooth brow and tug at her long hair. Her mouth wasn't large, but her lips were full. How old would she be? Not as old as him but perhaps in her late twenties? Was she beautiful? Yes, many people would have said so. Those big eyes, that smile. There was a wavy pattern in gold thread on the lower part of her sleeves. On her bosom, the gold was in the shape of a lily. It went well with the cherry-coloured dress. When Richard spoke to Leopold, it was in a mixture of French and German. They knew enough of each other's language to be able to converse. But with this nun he could speak his native tongue. He thought in French. Now that there was no need to translate what was in his mind, he immediately felt easier.

For three whole years—ever since he'd arrived in the Holy Land and right up to the present moment—he'd constantly been articulating his thoughts in a hybrid language that was a mixture of French, German, Latin, Flemish and English—the Crusaders' language. He looked fixedly at Anne. He thought she could hardly help noticing it.

Anne had a pleasant voice. A shade deeper than one might have expected in her slender frame. The day after they left Dürnstein, she had told of her childhood in a village in the Loire Valley. Her family was well-to-do. Convent life hadn't been a vocation for her. Her parents had given her, like a tithe, to the Church. Richard was surprised at her relating this without any kind of regret or reproach. She appeared to accept as providence that *she* among her siblings was to be the tithe and that she'd been chosen to fulfil God's plan and be a nun. The manner in which she'd acquiesced in her parents' choice made him see that they shared a common destiny. He felt sympathy for her and respect for the dignity she displayed when talking about her fate.

When the carriage drew up in front of the emperor's castle at Tiefels, the cords round Richard's hands and feet were removed. Leopold accompanied Richard to the emperor who was waiting outside for them at the other end of the castle yard. Anne walked a pace behind them.

The emperor approached.

'King Richard I of England, how strange that our first meeting should take place under such circumstances,' he said in a French that revealed more of a desire than an ability to speak it.

'So you don't recall that we met after the battle of Acre? I managed to greet you one of the few times you were outside your tent,' Richard said.

Inside the courtroom Richard was arraigned for the murder of Count Conrad of Montferrat. According to Leopold, Richard had killed Conrad because he was jealous of the one man capable of crushing Saladin and taking Jerusalem.

'The pope will judge King Richard harshly,' Emperor Henry said and looked out across the assembly that was made up of his household.

10

'Why is no cardinal or other emissary from the pope here?' Richard asked.

Too many witnesses were present for the question to be ignored. The split second it took Leopold and Henry to exchange glances to decide which of them would reply was enough to tell Richard that they'd been bluffing.

'You have no, I repeat, *no* authority from the pope, and you know it. I have received a message without your knowledge,' Richard lied.

Leopold and Henry looked doubtfully at one another.

'Did you know that Hubert Walter, my privy counsellor, and His Holiness the Pope had a meeting last week? Hubert Walter is not merely a bishop but also a handpicked papal envoy.'

When he saw the uncertainty in the faces before him, he was unstoppable.

'Your greed surpasses all bounds, but the fact that you have invoked the pope and God won't be tolerated by either of them.'

Leopold spoke. 'There's not much left of you now, Richard. Was there ever such a fall in history? Caesar, Pilate, perhaps, well even, yes . . . Judas Iscariot.'

'It's Philip who's pulling the strings. You and Philip met at Acre and made your plans. I know you,' Richard shouted, before being led out by five guards.

When fifty thousand marks, a third of ransom for Richard's head, had arrived at Regensburg, the trial was suspended.

Richard felt his strength returning. Revenge was nigh. He began to feel something akin to joy.

Leopold wanted the whole of the ransom before Richard was released. Henry thought they should content themselves with what they'd got. The emperor's opinion outranked the duke's.

Leopold got his share of the advance and prepared for the return journey. Four carriages were made ready to transport Richard and four servants home to Anjou.

Richard realized that he still needed the nun's help. He liked her, too. He heard her asking the duke when she would receive the money for her convent. Leopold said he didn't know what she was talking about. Richard confronted him and said that he needed her the whole way back to Anjou. They were to leave next morning and he would pay all she'd been promised, and more besides, if she came along.

Anne looked at him, curtsied and said it would be an honour. Leopold shrugged.

From his bedchamber in the east tower of the emperor's castle Richard could see the red sun resting on a blanket of mist. He was able to breakfast before being escorted to the

closed carriage that was to take him home. He seated himself comfortably in the pigskin seat, rested his head and
closed his eyes. Had his mother and Hubert Walter raised
the money only to punish him later? Would they have
preferred him to kill himself so they wouldn't have had to
find the money? No, that couldn't be. They needed him
against Philip and John. How was Berengaria? Did she
miss him? Why should she? He was the king. Any sort of
love was a handicap for a king chosen by God. It must be
the way God wanted it to be.

He felt pains in his neck and the beginnings of a
headache. Had Saladin, al-Adil and the nun understood
that his pains, whether in his limbs or in other parts of his
body, were often linked to what was going on in his head?
What caused mind and body to affect each other?

There was a knocking on the carriage door. Anne
appeared. She carried a roll of parchment under her arm.

'A messenger delivered this to the duke early this
morning. It's for you.'

III
ROUEN

The morning light discovered the skeleton of a bush. The scab of the moon had vanished, a snake awoke in the brush behind a desiccated prickly pear. Heaven and earth met in a razor-sharp line far ahead, archipelagos of cloud glided above the sand and the scrub and the occasional sun-parched olive bush. The horses' hooves clattered over the brittle slate of the dried-up stream bed.

They halted at the remains of a fire. Flies buzzed in the hot air. Between pieces of charcoal lay the remains of two soldiers. Close by something stirred. Two vultures hacked at half a horse that lay on its side. He picked up a stone and hurled it at the great birds. They took no notice of him. Only after the third stone did they clumsily flap their grey and black wings a couple of times, without taking off. The eyes were the only parts of their small, wet heads that weren't bloody.

A little way off stood a cart resting on its shafts. Before them lay sand, just completely featureless sand.

1

> *Dear Richard, I'm longing to see you. What a relief to know that I shall meet you in this life. Wasn't that what I told you? Everything in your chamber is untouched. Even Charlemagne's sword hangs above your writing table. Everything here is in perfect order. Except that you aren't with us. How we shall celebrate!*

Richard read the words on the parchment several times. He couldn't sleep. At last he could go home, ride wherever he wanted, see that landscape he'd thought so much about, sit with his mother, talk, joke and laugh, receive visitors, have poets perform for him, write himself... Well, one could always dream. For a moment Richard tried to convince himself that he had no responsibilities in this world. He tried again and again.

It was in vain. He upbraided himself for possessing a mind that could shape such meaningless notions.

Now and again he glanced at the nun who was sitting directly opposite him. Her eyes were closed. Richard doubted she was asleep. They were inside a closed carriage with room for four. Although the convoy was moving quickly, the journey to the Anjou border would take several days. The route lay along the Danube to Swabia. After that they'd have to cross the Rhine, the Seine and the Loire, and then follow the Loire until they reached his mother's castle at Anger.

Eleanor had been Richard's regent in England during his absence. She'd have filled the position well, no doubt. She didn't complain in her letter at any rate. He knew that she wasn't the sort of person to worry him unnecessarily.

The nun's mild presence soothed Richard. He looked at the hair fringing her forehead. He followed the line of her arched eyelids. He thought of boats and half-moons. Her job at the convent wasn't only to grow the herbs but to process and prepare the plants. Her earrings swung back and forth as the carriage moved on. They were made of a large, gold-mounted pearl to which was attached two links holding a lesser pearl and an emerald.

'Have you been on a pilgrimage to Jerusalem?' Richard asked.

The nun opened her eyes and fixed him with her lavender-blue gaze.

She nodded.

He regretted his question.

She talked about Jerusalem. Of all the towers, the domes, the Via Dolorosa, Golgotha, the Dome of the Rock on the Temple Mount, mosques, churches and synagogues, the Holy Sepulchre, the olive trees and the city wall. He nodded. He couldn't remember the last time anyone had spoken to him with such a joy and conviction of beauty. He could hear his own breathing. When she'd finished speaking, she looked directly at him. She clearly expected him to say something. Couldn't she just have carried on all the way back to Anjou? He began to describe the Mount of Olives, with its view of the Holy City. He had been there. A strange name, of course, but did she know the reason for it? The mountain was called the Mount of Olives because for centuries there had been an olive press there. Huge quantities of olive oil had been produced on the Mount of Olives. Did she know that? He noticed she was studying him.

'But the Mount of Olives isn't its actual name,' he added quickly. 'It's the *Mountain of the Olive Trees*. It's so beautiful there.'

She nodded. He spoke of the thick, gnarled trees with their long, thin leaves that glittered like silver in the wind. He had stood on the summit of the mount. There was a small church on the spot where Jesus had ascended. And he had even taken a walk through the Garden of Gethsemane as the sun was setting, past the Sepulchre, and seen 'the Golden City'. Richard talked about how Jesus had been betrayed in this lovely garden and how the traitor Judas had hanged himself on one of its olive trees.

'The traitor,' Richard mumbled.

She looked enquiringly at him.

He started to describe the Christian, Muslim, Armenian and Jewish quarters of Jerusalem, repeating the portrait de Sablé had painted for him. What would he say if she asked whether he'd followed the route Jesus took, through the narrow alleys along the Via Dolorosa? From the Mount of Olives he'd been able to make out several parts of the city, after de Sablé had pointed them out and described them. The Armenian quarter and the Temple of the Rock weren't difficult to spot, the rest he'd simply imagined. He'd seen everything from afar, the Holy City directly below and in front of him to the left, the Judaean Desert and the valley of Gehenna. Nearly every night he was haunted by the view from the top of the Mount of Olives. He knew that the Via Dolorosa wasn't a river of gold in which floated thorns from Jesus' crown and nails that had been hammered through His feet and hands but, rather, a narrow, bustling commercial street where bargaining, swindling and theft went on at all hours of the day, surrounded by the stench of dust, dung and urine. He hadn't seen it with himself but there was no reason to doubt the men who'd been there on their way to Saladin.

He wasn't lying to her.

'Did you meet King Lalibela?' Anne enquired.

'Who?'

'The king of Ethiopia. He's so black his skin is almost blue. He was in Jerusalem when you were there.'

'I only spoke to the faithful.'

'He was there as a pilgrim. He is a believer. Did you know that he's made an underground model of Jerusalem in his own country, carved out of stone? He constructed six churches, including the Church of the Holy Sepulchre, just like their originals. A host of angels carved it out, helped by the king, over the course of several days and nights.'

Richard smiled.

'I've met nuns who've seen Little Jerusalem,' she said.

He saw she was piqued.

2

'Why did you leave the Holy Land?'

Anne raised the question Richard least wanted to hear.

Smoke was rising from the fire, blowing towards him. Richard rubbed his eyes. The smoke changed direction. Anne was standing directly in front of him.

'I had to go home because of my brother John. I gave him considerable land and property before joining the Crusade, but I'm afraid he won't be satisfied with that. He may well have formed an alliance with King Philip.'

'So John is more important than the fight against the Saracens?'

Her face was placid, he couldn't detect anything reminiscent of reproach in it.

'John's greed could ruin the entire English Kingdom. If he succeeds, another Crusade would be out of the question. I need a strong army and money to lead this holy war.'

Anne leant towards him.

'Remember what the apostle Paul says in his Second Letter to the Corinthians: "Therefore I take pleasure in my infirmities, in reproaches, in necessities, in persecutions, in distresses, for Christ's sake: for when I am weak, then I am strong.'"

'Are you saying I'm weak?' Richard said exasperated.

'Aren't we all weak at least once in our lives? Most of us are not so courageous as Paul the leper. He turned his weakness into strength. And because he was sick God spoke through him.'

'But what's this got to do with me?'

'We never see God so clearly as when we look into the face of the one we despise and detest,' she went on. 'God *is* in the weak, the scorned, the ugly, the loathsome and the hideous. He is there in your weaknesses.'

Richard didn't understand what she meant. He was silent.

As they crossed into Anjou, mist and rain descended. On the horizon were the outlines of forests and wooded hills. Richard recognized the smell of drying mushrooms. The peasants in the large fields a little way off bent slightly into the wind as they walked. Later in the morning the weather improved and his party decided to travel on. Richard heard the sound of horses' hooves on the cart track a little distance off. Shortly after, six riders came galloping up. Five were in uniform. There was little doubt about their identity. The man in the lead held Richard's banner. The sixth rider obviously wasn't a soldier.

'Hubert! Why are you here?'

Hubert Walter was dressed in a brown bishop's habit. He had a cross round his neck.

'You seem uninjured, Richard. Thanks be to God. The Lord be praised.'

'Why are you here? Has anything happened to my mother? Has John chased you out of England?'

'I've just had a meeting with Eleanor. We've been discussing how we should work together to get Philip out of Normandy.'

'How much has he gained control of?'

'A bit more than a quarter, but he's on the back foot.'

'How did you and my mother get on?'

'You mean your regent?' said Hubert Walter smiling. 'I have the impression that she's satisfied with the way I carry out her orders.'

'You haven't changed, you still can't answer with a clear yes or no. Have you said anything to her about Jerusalem?'

'Shall we just agree to say as little as possible?'

'Was that what you came to say?'

'The world needs heroes more than ever.'

'Why aren't you in England fighting John?'

'The situation is under control.'

'Is John dead?'

Walter shook his head.

Richard took the bridle and helped him out of the saddle and asked him into the carriage.

Richard introduced Anne and Walter to one another. The carriage began to move and she soon fell asleep.

Walter nodded towards Anne.

'Talk away, Walter.'

'John was terrified when he learnt you were to be set free, Richard. He quickly realized that he'd never be able to steal the Crown from you,' Hubert Walter said quietly.

'I assume he's been aided by that coterie of nobles who supported my father but never supported the Crusade?'

'Almost all of them have fled now. No sooner had Eleanor and I raised your ransom than there were rebellions in all his domains. He's lost most of what you gave him before you left for the Holy Land. I have control of England. You don't need to go there immediately.'

'That's kind of you, Hubert, but I am the country's king. We're talking about a couple of dozen counts?'

'Two.'

'Are you saying that to put my mind at rest?'

'Only Tickhill and Nottingham are left. Our men got new strength once they heard you'd been released.'

'I want to go to England to subdue the rest of the opposition.'

Richard began to talk about the rain and the fog and what time they would reach Anger. Soon they began discussing the newly chosen pope, Clement III, and what advantage there was in the fact that Hubert Walter had known him for many years.

'So it's not true that Leopold had meetings with the pope?' Richard asked.

'They never took place. Do you know what the pope said about Leopold in Rome recently? That "the duke is one of the coarsest fellows who ever lived. No crime can be worse than imprisoning our finest Crusader and making money out of it."'

Walter glanced over at Anne to make certain she was still asleep before whispering:

'I went to your mother to get permission to execute John.' Walter drew breath. 'But she said no.'

Anne opened her eyes.

Just then it dawned on Richard that they would soon part.

'Will you join my retinue for the next few months? I need you. The near future will be very tough and I'm anxious about my health. As regards the money I owe you and your convent, I will send what I promised. I'll pay you double if you say yes.'

'Yes,' she said, without hesitation.

3

He'd never felt so worried before any battle as he did before meeting his mother. Had she become frail? Was she as sharp as she had been? Did Hubert hold sway over her? Where Hubert was clever and formal, she was direct, unequivocal and anything but tactical, or at least she had been up to now.

Richard caught sight of his mother as the carriage turned up to the wide steps. She was standing outside waving to him. In her right hand she held her stick. She shouted to him while he was still inside the carriage. He didn't hear what she said. The entire court was present as well as others from Anjou and the surrounding domains. The commander of the guards, the servants, the old doctor, the cooks, the bakers, the huntsmen, the smith, the cartwright and many others whom he did not know. They were all dressed in their finery. They cheered and eyed him with admiration. Just behind the representatives of the court were seven men and women wearing home-spun woollen clothes. The women had headscarves. The clouds were grey and black. An icy wind had gradually made its presence felt that morning. Richard recognized two of the people staring at him. They were Jacques and Sara Breton.

'We got permission to come, Your Majesty. Congratulations on your victory over the Saracens and the conquest of Jerusalem. Is the city made of pure gold?' Jacques enquired.

'Have you brought a piece along?' asked Sara.

Richard shook his head and gave a wry smile. He glanced at the castle steps. Where was his mother? He hadn't noticed Berengaria. A grey, four-legged creature stood before him.

'But isn't this . . .'

'No, it's not Wolf,' Jacques cut in. 'This is his son. We heard from Queen Eleanor that your old dog is dead. But we've been looking after Wolf II.'

The dog sat down obediently next to Jacques.

'Some dogs are as wise as their owners. And that's true, because I've got one here,' said Jacques.

'By "owner" he means you, Your Majesty, because from now on he's yours,' said Sara.

'He likes you, can you see? He's laughing with his tail,' said Jacques. 'You can't force a dog to wag its tail.'

'When Odysseus returned from Troy, only his dog recognized him,' said Richard.

'You seem to be better remembered,' Sara said.

Richard felt a tap on the back. His mother was approaching with a lady-in-waiting on each side.

'We haven't been very lucky with the weather, mother,' Richard said.

'All this talk about the weather—why doesn't anyone do something about it?'

She handed her stick to the nearer of the ladies and embraced her son. He felt her thin, strong arms around his body. She was older, certainly, but she was looking well.

'Do you know, these people . . .' She nodded at the two Bretons. '. . . They've given all their savings so that we could ransom you.'

'Thank you,' said Richard and bowed to Jacques and Sara. 'Whatever you've given me, you shall have returned.'

Richard and his mother climbed the steps. The others followed.

Did it look as if she were proud of him?

'Had you heard that Duke Leopold is dead?'

Her face shone with pleasure. She laughed and clenched her bony fists. The previous day a messenger had arrived with news of the duke's fate.

The Viennese court had tried to keep the news quiet for as long as possible—the duke had been riding down the hills from Dürnstein to the Danube and was talking to his aides about his son's forthcoming wedding. As he was speaking, his horse was alarmed by a sudden report. The horse threw him and bolted.

In Vienna it was said that the duke had injured himself jousting. His age and his lack of ability as a rider caused the story to be largely disbelieved. Rumour had spread throughout the courts of Europe that Leopold had been excommunicated by the pope. The duke had lost more and more friends. The fall from his horse was seen as a sign from above. This opinion wasn't weakened when he got gangrene. The doctors thought his leg would have to be cut off. If one waited too long, gangrene would develop in the other leg as well. There was disagreement among the doctors about where to amputate. Leopold lost patience. He did it himself with the help of a servant and an axe. The axe had to be wielded three times before the leg was severed from the body. On his deathbed, Leopold made amends to the pope, was given the last rights and asked the bishop, who was standing at his bedside, to convey his deeply felt regrets to Richard and Pope Clement.

Richard's mother kissed him on both cheeks.

'You look a bit older, my son.'

'I've got a few wrinkles.'

'They mean nothing.'

'I've got a bit of a stomach.'

'That doesn't mean anything either.'

'Imprisonment has probably changed me in ways it's possible to see.'

'You ought to have a son, Richard. Do you think this "nun" you've brought with you can help?'

'She really is a nun and she's helped me with herbs and medicines.'

'You're not telling me she's a virgin, too?'

'I've no reason to think otherwise.'

Eleanor raised her head and looked over at Anne Hofer.

'She's beautiful.'

'You know that I'm married, Mother?'

Eleanor was wearing a long, black gown which covered almost the whole of her pale form, apart from her hands and throat. Richard studied the thin face. It had always been difficult to spy changes in it, whether she was happy or weighed down with sorrow. She received every type of news impassively. Was that how she had survived everything?

'Mother, I must speak to you alone.'

'That's fine, we'll go to my rooms.'

She beckoned the two ladies-in-waiting who were quickly at her side. As they left the hall there was applause and everyone shouted 'Long live King Richard, the conqueror and saviour of Jerusalem!'

Richard blushed as he walked a couple of paces behind his mother and the two ladies-in-waiting.

His mother was walking more slowly than she had the last time he'd seen her and she also dragged her right foot a little. As he listened to the brief instructions his mother gave to her helpers who were guiding her down the long passage, he had a sense of relief and security. She wasn't angry with him. She didn't look censorious. She'd said nothing about what he'd done at Acre with the people he'd roped together, not a word about his humiliation at Ascalon. She hadn't even mentioned Jerusalem. So perhaps the rumours hadn't preceded him after all?

There was a directness in the way she talked to him which convinced him that everything was as it had been, when he and his mother hadn't just been mother and son but intimate as only close friends can be.

His mother seated herself on the four-poster bed, dismissed the ladies-in-waiting and whispered, 'Shh.'

She opened the drawer of her bedside table and brought out his gold ring which she'd received from Duke Leopold. She put it on his finger.

'It looks good,' said Eleanor, 'It's just been polished.'

Her face shone, without reserve. It struck him that she looked like a woman who had finally got the child she'd been waiting for and was pouring out over him the loneliness of her past. In this closed universe, she was the undisputed ruler and he the subject.

'Is it true that you refused to let Hubert Walter and his men execute John?' Richard asked.

Eleanor looked at him for some time before replying. It was probably because the light was falling from an oblique and favourable angle that he could see for the first time that her eyes weren't merely green but had a strain of brown in them around the pupils.

'He has done you much harm, Richard. A great deal of harm. But he is my son. Certainly not my favourite son, as you well know. But as a mother, I beg you to spare him.'

'I'm the king. His treachery deserves a dozen death sentences.'

'I've got a present for you,' she said, smiling secretively. 'I was given them some years ago by Count Raymond of Tripoli, now they are yours.'

Eleanor summoned her ladies-in-waiting. A cage was carried across to Richard.

'They're the slowest animals in the world,' she said.

Richard tried to make out legs under the heavy shells. The biggest one stretched out a skinny, whitish-grey head of tiny grey scales. Its eyes were barely open beneath the silky eyelids. A crack of a mouth chomped at the lettuce leaves before it and they vanished noiselessly into its head.

'Are you teasing me? Do you remember the troubadours and jesters who compared Philip and me to tortoises because we took so long to set out for the Holy Land?'

'They were right, weren't they? Perhaps you can be quicker in your Normandy war with Philip? He's no great warrior, but don't underestimate him. I hope the tortoises will stimulate you.'

'There's something I have to confess.'

'Don't worry about that now, you've had enough to contend with.'

'I could have done things better.'

'You are a rock. Times are different now. Do you recall ancient Heraclitus' words about how you can never step into one and the same river twice? Richard, now is the time to gain control of England and the British Isles and the *whole* of France, even the part that Philip rules. I have begun to plan it in detail.'

Richard embraced her again: 'My strength is intact.'

'I was worried that your time at Dürnstein might have robbed you of your fighting spirit.'

'Don't be uneasy. I'm the same man the pope's envoy called upon to take the Cross. With head and body, with my whole being, I was moving towards one goal, towards Jerusalem. This time the war will be fought in our landscape, in our climate, with no debilitating sun to hamper me. As a warrior, Philip is a mediocrity compared to Saladin. But, Mother, where is Berengaria?'

'She's been visiting her relatives in Navarre these past six months.'

'When does she return?'

'In a few months.'

4

Richard gazed across the newly ploughed fields. At their margin he saw the forest's side and the gentle slopes of maples and pines where he'd ridden out so often, sometimes with a lance in his hand and sometimes not. A little way off, a man was hauling a heavy cart along the muddy track. The wheels sank deep into the ruts. The clouds chased each other across the sky. The man waved. Richard turned, there was no one else in sight. Richard waved back. Was it Jacques Breton? The man didn't get far before he stopped again. Maybe the cart was full of stones that he'd managed to lever up with a bar in the hope of winning a little arable land? It had rained the whole of the previous night. Richard had lain sleepless because of his mother's words the evening before. The river was in spate below the mill. Fallen branches came down in the torrent, touched and tangled with each other. A large twig turned and was lifted clear of the water like a dark hand. He inhaled. This was his landscape, it was a part of him. To his right, beside a gate, he could see a flock of sheep and a long-legged brown dog. It harboured no doubts about its own importance, appearance, position or aims. It ran ceaselessly among the flighty sheep, shepherding them in through the gate. Sometimes it barked to command respect, at others it ran over to a man who had appeared on the right. He must be its master. The dog looked confidently at him, its imploring eyes begging for a contented look or a pat. Richard smiled and felt peace settling on him. Had the feeling been the same when he'd looked at the landscape as a boy? Had it looked like this when Jesus was alive? It wasn't death itself he'd feared most in the Holy Land or in Dürnstein, but the thought that he might never see the landscape of his childhood again.

Just inside the main door of the castle he made out a figure in the semi-darkness. It was Anne. Had she been watching him? Had he been talking to himself? If so, might she have caught a word or two?

He looked down at the flagstones, took a few steps, put his arms behind his back and paced round her in a circle. He noticed that she stood still, following him with her eyes. Did she think him a fine man? Perhaps she considered it a sinful thought? Her waist seemed slender beneath the long, dark blue dress with its red embroidery. He halted before going a step closer. She stood still. He noticed her breath and found it pleasant. Richard's right hand couldn't have been closer to her left one without touching it.

He studied her eyes. He couldn't see any trace of animosity in them.

'Sister Anne, when you were in Jerusalem on your pilgrimage, when did you feel closest to Jesus Christ and our Lord?'

She met his gaze.

'For three days I followed in Jesus' footsteps along the Via Dolorosa, where he'd carried the Cross, and each time

I could hear our Lord speaking to me. I felt a great rage against those who had derided and tortured our saviour Jesus Christ. When I stood beneath the Ecce Homo Arch, where Pontius Pilate displayed Jesus wearing a crown of thorns and a purple robe, as he bled from wounds all over his body, I heard Pilate's raucous voice: "Behold the man." Our Saviour fell for the first time just there and, immediately, he saw his mother.'

'Have you seen the cloth that was used to wipe the blood and sweat from Jesus' face?'

'Oh, yes . . . and then, after a turn to the right, he fell for the second time.'

Anne shut her eyes. '"Weep not for me, but weep for yourselves, and for your children," he said to the women on either side of him. Have you seen the place where his so-called crimes were proclaimed? According to Roman custom, Jesus would have had another chance to live if just a single person in the crowd had requested it. No one said a word. No one. What cowards we are. No one. Cowardice is our scourge. It is our cross.'

'But the Church of the Holy Sepulchre . . .'

'When the daylight was almost gone, I went into the holiest of all churches. Can you guess who I met on the Via Dolorosa a couple of years before you arrived there? Yes, it was Saladin.'

Richard opened his eyes wide. 'You're lying.'

'We met him on his way to the al-Aqsa Mosque. There were four of us nuns, he asked us where we were going. He was walking with two bodyguards. I was with Helena, one of our nuns, who can speak both Latin and

Arabic. He asked if we had prayed in the Church of the Holy Sepulchre.'

'Was he wearing a turban shot through with gold thread? Did he have a scarlet tunic and a sabre encrusted with gemstones?'

'He looked like a tailor. He went bareheaded.'

'But surely you can't doubt that Saladin was dangerous?'

Richard saw that she was angry.

'And what does Hubert Walter think of Saladin?'

'What's he got to do with it?'

'I suppose you know that he visited the sultan while you were in Dürnstein?'

'What?'

'I learnt it from the duke himself. He said he'd informed the pope of Walter's visit, without receiving any reply. You look surprised?'

Richard straightened his blue velvet cloak and pushed the hair out of his eyes.

'I'm not going to discuss this with you,' he said.

'I talked to your mother yesterday. She was very kind to me. She complimented me on my clothes and my French,' she said.

Suppose it hadn't been a miracle that Saladin changed his mind and refused to let his archers kill him at Ascalon. Could Saladin have decided that for himself without the help of God? They had taken aim. He wouldn't have stood a chance.

'I think I'll go, Sire. You obviously have things on your mind,' Anne said.

Richard nodded and followed her out. It was dark now. She took her leave, he mumbled some reply he immediately forgot. He looked up at the stars, at Pisces' mouth, which stretched right down to the harbours of light in the valley. It wasn't inconceivable that, by sparing him, Saladin imagined Richard would interpret it as magnanimity towards a fallen enemy, a gallant gesture without risk. That the rumour might spread throughout Europe and everyone would realize that Richard wasn't invincible. Had Duke Leopold been partly right after all? But to Richard it didn't make sense. If Saladin had killed him, most of the knights would have left for home even sooner. Wasn't it he who'd bolstered their morale and enabled his knights to last out so long?

Queen Eleanor invited her son to breakfast. They were alone, with just one servant in attendance. His mother shook as she helped herself. Even with the servant's help she had difficulty in getting the food to her mouth. Her age was affecting her more than he'd realized. Though she wore a large bib she soiled the black dress she'd been wearing the previous day. He made no comment about it. Nor the fact that it was the first time he'd seen her wear the same clothes two days in a row.

'Are you disappointed in me, Mother?'

Her eyes took on a dull lustre. Her mouth pursed. She turned her head away from him, got up with difficulty, walked a few stiff paces on her unsupple hips, so as not to seize up completely, as she put it, before sitting down again and staring at him.

'If you'd brought Saladin's head home with you, the world would have looked quite different.'

'I haven't lost my ability. I'm not as weak and cowardly as John. I will kill Philip and we will rule England and all of France.'

'I've tried to defend our borders against Philip with the help of men I could trust. Did Hubert Walter tell you?' Eleanor asked.

'You led our army against Philip?'

'Well, you were far away.'

'Mother, did you want me to return from the Crusade at the same time as Philip?'

'I needed you here.'

'But you wanted me to lead the Crusade?'

'For God's, the pope's and all our sakes—yes. And, once you'd killed the Antichrist, England and the whole of France would have been yours. If you'd taken Saladin as soon as you had the opportunity, we wouldn't have had problems here at home.'

'Don't you think I'm capable of taking Normandy any more?'

Eleanor raised her head and fixed him with meek eyes.

'You'll see that I'm worthy of being your son. I shall plunge my sword into Philip a hundred times.'

His mother studied his face and said mildly, 'Once will be enough.'

5

Richard flung open Hubert Walter's door. Hubert was still in bed. Richard stood at the bed's foot.

'I am the King of England.'

Hubert Walter rubbed his eyes.

'Naturally.'

'You are my official. I shall go to England tomorrow and show my subjects that I'm alive and that the king is the one who has the real power. If I don't go, they may think it's you who rules the land. Has this thought never struck you?'

Hubert Walter shook his head.

'I shall personally inflict John's final defeat.'

'England has never had a better ruler than you, Richard.'

On 11 March 1194, as Richard and Hubert Walter were about to set sail for England, Anne Hofer asked if they would be away for long and why the king didn't need her help. He replied that his stay would be so short that it wouldn't be required.

'But there's chaos in the land, isn't there?' she asked, astonished.

'No, that's something the king believes,' said Hubert Walter, bowing gallantly.

As soon as they arrived at Sandwich on 13 March, they rode to Canterbury to hold a memorial service for Thomas à Becket.

The following week they were in Nottingham with almost a thousand soldiers. The sandy roads lay ochre yellow before them, the ploughed fields stretched dark brown to the horizon. A thunderstorm was on its way. They encountered no resistance. Most of John's men at Nottingham had fled long before. John had told the remainder that he would return within a few days.

When Richard's retinue arrived at the castle, he gave orders for the royal horn-and-trumpet fanfare. The defenders of the fortress were convinced it was a trick. Richard's men rode to the moat and called on the occupiers to surrender. The officer on the wall gave orders to shoot and to set fire to everything combustible round the castle walls. Shortly afterwards, Richard and his men took four prisoners. They were hanged by the drawbridge that led to the main gate of the fortress. No sooner had the noose tightened round the neck of the fourth prisoner than burning arrows hailed down on the besiegers. Richard and Walter rode up to the walls. Walter was holding the banner.

'Do you realize that you're making war on Richard I, England's only true king?' Richard shouted.

Walter translated his words into English.

'Well, show us this king!' came the shouted reply.

Walter translated into French.

'C'est moi,' Richard roared.

Walter pointed at Richard.

'He's in the Holy Land!' was the shout, before arrows once again rained down on Richard and his men. The next prisoners weren't hanged but taken to Richard's tent to see the crown, sceptre and sword of state lying on a table. The prisoners were sent back to the fortress where they could vouch for the fact that they'd met King Richard himself. Shortly after, the white flag fluttered over the castle. When the survivors surrendered, they were given safe conduct and ordered to pay large fines.

Only now could Richard be certain that all resistance in England had been quelled. He sent most of his soldiers back to London that same afternoon.

The next day Richard and Walter travelled through Sherwood Forest with a large retinue of followers. They were on their way to London to hold a ceremony that would signal the beginning of the war with Philip. Before them rode forty soldiers and standard bearers. Behind them came cooks, cupbearers, grooms, chamberlains, jesters, harlequins, servants and an assorted body of people who were hoping for an audience with the king. The weather was pleasant and mild. Richard gave orders to make camp. He went out hunting, taking four of his best huntsmen with him. There wasn't a soul to be seen in the great deciduous forest. They felled a stag with bow and arrow. A thrush and a dove avoided the hunters' aim.

That evening a messenger arrived with the news that John had fled to France.

Richard told Walter that he would triple the size of the army and take the whole of Normandy and neighbouring Vexin, which belonged to Philip. Walter was silent.

'My mother and I intend to conquer the whole of France.'

'Can't we do one thing at a time?'

'That's an order.'

Walter didn't answer.

'Friends should be honest with each other, Hubert, don't you agree?'

'Yes.'

'Why didn't you tell me that you'd met Saladin?'

Richard noticed that Walter avoided his eyes. His answer was long in coming.

'You remember that you enjoined me to arrange an "organized, tactical retreat" with the military command?'

Walter was breathing heavily.

'I wanted to see if there was anything in the rumours that Saladin's army would cross the Mediterranean and attack north of the Alps.'

'What did he say?'

'"We don't fight wars of conquest." Also, I thought it sensible to speak to Saladin to avoid any attack when our army was boarding ship for its journey home. Imagine if they'd shot at us with the siege machines we left behind?'

'And so you asked our knights to negotiate a truce?'

'Yes.'

'That's not correct. We controlled the harbour at Acre. It was impossible for the Saracen forces to shoot at us from the rear and, as for the siege machines, I gave orders that they be destroyed. You're lying, Hubert, or should we say that, for once, you're being slightly too economical?'

When the coachmen asked if they were to stop at Leicester for food, Richard gave an emphatic no. He wanted to get to London as soon as possible. They were given instructions to get food they could carry with them and ride on. For most of the journey Richard sat and looked out of the carriage, or slept to avoid seeing Walter's face.

As they approached London, Richard opened his eyes.

'You're not fearful for your life, Hubert?'

Hubert Walter shrugged his shoulders.

Richard slapped him.

Walter raised his hand to his red cheek. He looked surprised.

'When you were employed by my father, you hadn't any scruples about working for his greatest enemy.'

'I don't understand.'

'You were the one who brought my mother's letters to me when she was in prison. If we're being technical, couldn't that be seen as obvious treachery towards the king you were serving at the time?'

'Mightn't it have been in your father's interest that they got to you?'

'Don't try to be clever. Why shouldn't you be disloyal to my mother and me as well? You did my mother a service because you realized that my father would die soon.'

'What can I do to gain your approbation?'

'I'm going to declare all-out war on Philip, I depend on your full support.'

'That will be expensive, and I think several important allies will be against us.'

'Not if you say that it will strengthen our finances in the long term.'

'I'm not sure if that argument is correct.'

This was quite a different Hubert Walter to the one he'd employed as his closest adviser before he set sail for Acre. There was no bowing and scraping now. He seemed arrogant and unafraid. Did he need Hubert in order to take Normandy? Could he manage without him? Unfortunately not.

'I'll be interested to hear what my mother has to say when I tell her about our conversation.'

Possibly Hubert's eyes showed a trace of discernible fear, but not as much as Richard had hoped for. Hubert's cheek was still a flaming red.

They drove directly to Westminster Palace. When the carriage stopped, Hubert rose quickly, bowed and left to continue his journey to Winchester where, in his capacity as archbishop of Canterbury, he was to prepare for the following week's big ceremony in the cathedral. The Church was to signal its support for Richard's war with Philip.

When Richard got out of the carriage, he felt unsteady. He clutched the door, before taking a few tentative steps. His servant and one of the coachmen steadied him. Richard shook them off. He almost fell. Two birds flew right over him. The bells in the palace chapel rang out three times. He looked down at his knees. His legs kept him upright. The toes of his boots were pointing in the right direction for the main door. His knees began to tremble. The birds vanished. Could he hear wingbeats? Were the birds returning? He began to walk, one foot in front of the other. He knew how to pull himself together. He didn't lie down. Certainly not. He could see. He could count and talk. Hubert must realize that he and his mother would strike, suddenly.

6

The coachmen enquired whether they shouldn't do a tour of London before starting out for Winchester Cathedral.

'We can drive the whole length of the Strand, past Somerset House, so that you can view the fine panorama across the Thames, Sire. And just before the Tower you can see Southwark. It's beautiful there. Did you know London has twenty-five thousand inhabitants?' said the eldest coachman proudly.

'Drive straight to Winchester.'

The stench from the Thames was abominable. Richard wondered if the English had learnt to bury their dead.

The market had little to offer compared to its counterpart in Anger. But by the standards of the market in Jericho, it had a lot. Here in London they sold fish from the Thames! People queued up to buy it! Hens and lambs ran about inside an enclosure before they were slaughtered. Two animal-tamers were parading a large, tame black bear on a chain. A fire-eater breathed flames at Richard as he stuck his head out of the carriage. From what he'd heard, far too much of the population migrated to London from all over England. Hubert Walter ought to put a stop to it.

The only reason Richard was in the city was that he needed the Londoners' support for his war in Normandy. Just think, he'd once said he would sell London to get money for the Crusade. Only now did he realize just what a small sacrifice it would have been. Hubert Walter was in charge of the ceremony at Winchester which would set in train the war that he clearly didn't support as wholeheartedly as Richard and his mother. Walter had tried to get out of the job, but Richard refused.

The solid main doors of the cathedral were opened by two monks just before the High Mass. It was 15 April, the first Sunday after Easter. The nobility, officials and eminent burghers were invited to a ceremony never before witnessed in that great cathedral. Five years earlier, the same people had attended Richard's coronation.

When the seats and standing room were taken, the doors were shut. Once the sun stood in the middle of the sky, the royal fanfare sounded. Richard strode in with his crown, sceptre and purple cloak.

Queen Berengaria hadn't been invited. Eleanor was at Richard's side, with her stick and unsteady gait, and she, too, wore a crown and a cape of dyed fur. Just as they entered the cathedral he whispered to her:

'Hubert Walter is trying to seize power, Mother.'

'He's been a great help to both of us,' she said out loud.

'Do you know who he talked to in Jerusalem?' Richard whispered.

'This will be a wonderful day, my son,' Eleanor said and sat down.

Hubert Walter stood in front of the altar. The king and the dowager queen sat in the first row. On the other side was Anne Hofer. She was part of Eleanor's retinue which had arrived that same morning.

After another fanfare the service began. It ended in an ovation to the war, God and Richard, followed by the Gregorian choir's three songs prior to the recessional.

Richard stood up, made certain that his crown of gold and diamonds was in place, raised his sceptre, lifted his cloak so that he wouldn't trip and walked slowly down the central aisle. Eleanor was half a pace behind him. Next followed Hubert Walter and all the others. When the king reached the opened main doors, the royal fanfare sounded once more. The mass of humanity outside cheered Richard just as the sunlight dazzled him.

'What are they shouting, Hubert?'

'The people love you.'

The poet Bertran de Born was standing close by and called out in French:

'Long live our great king!'

Richard walked over to the poet. The man was a head shorter than himself but his hair was longer.

'Good poet, I wish you to write a few lines as an exhortation to my soldiers. In a few days we shall take Normandy.'

The poet went to it straight away. Next morning, Bertran de Born read out the following to Richard and Hubert Walter:

I tell you,
I find little joy
in food or wine or sleep,
compared to the cry of 'Get them'
on both sides of the line.
Oh, how I yearn
to hear the hooves of horses
who've lost their riders
and the cries of 'Help, help,'
and the sight of high and low falling to the grass,
into the ditches
and the dead with their
mortal wounds.
Take this lay to Lord
Yea and Nay,
and tell him that
for too long he has clung to
this clammy peace.

Richard patted the poet on the shoulder and gave him a handful of silver coins.

'"Lord Yea and Nay" is an extraordinary title to give our king,' said Walter.

The poet fixed his eyes on the marble tiles in the anteroom.

'Hubert, it shows that Bertran de Born is a true poet. He understands my soldiers and knows what they call me.'

'"Yea" and "Nay"?' Walter asked.

'You of all people ought to know that I'm a man of few words. It's my men who have given me the nickname. Haven't you realized that?'

'I've heard another interpretation of the words. And I've forbidden it.'

'Which?'

'In the Languedoc dialect they're said to mean abrupt and inconstant. Where do they get it from?' said Walter shaking his head.

The poet said his thanks and left them.

'I owe it to you to be honest, Richard. Good friends speak their minds openly one to another, isn't that what you always say? Yesterday, as you know, I was appointed justiciar, marshal and papal legate.'

'Speak!'

'The judges of the King's Bench and the officials at the Exchequer think that I should try to get you to moderate your preparations against the French. It will be too costly. "The king is waging war on France because of his reduced influence and position in England," said one of the lords who believes he represents the majority view.'

'Those wouldn't be your words, would they, Hubert?'

Walter cleared his throat.

'But criticism is also becoming more strident among influential tin-mine proprietors, in the wool trade and in the ports, too. There are even rumours that your own hand-picked men, Robert of Thornham and Geoffrey de la Celle, knights who followed you to the Holy Land, think that the war is not worth fighting any more.'

'Why?'

'Because they make more by trading than waging war.'

'Eleanor's and my ambition, my good clerk . . .' Richard spat out the words, ' . . . as you have always been well aware, is to complete the Norman conquest of England and the rest of the British Isles that was begun in 1066. The aim is to make the whole of France, England, Scotland, Ireland and Wales one. My father was too weak. I shall be king of that great realm. You will be the one who will give it life and make it function each and every day. But *I* am the ruler, not you. Remember that.'

'I'll support you, but how much time do you need?'

'Six months,' Richard replied, without hesitating.

On the morning of 2 May, Richard and his fleet of more than one hundred ships, tried to cross the Channel from Portsmouth. Experienced seafarers advised against setting out. The rocks in the harbour looked like a fleet which had weighed anchor. The furious azure-blue sea beat against their granite hulls. The gulls flew out across the water and formed an armada of white crosses. The waves got steadily higher and sharper. The wind increased in force. In the afternoon they had to turn back. Not until the evening of 12 May, after two months in England, did they set out. Once they were under way, Richard looked back at the crescent of shoreline in the moonlight before turning his gaze to the bow that was slicing the silken cloth of the sea. He couldn't remember a more pleasant sea journey. Next morning they went ashore near Cherbourg.

Richard jumped onto the wooden jetty and shouted:

'God has willed that we should return with our full force. Philip must abdicate or die. But first we'll deal with John.'

Richard heard that his voice was clear and insistent. He asked himself if he were shouting so loudly because he harboured a tiny seed of doubt. Not about whether he would manage to capture John, but about how he would defeat Philip. Philip was short of fighting experience, certainly, but he was cunning. That he had always been. He wasn't unprepared. The mere fact that Richard asked himself the question reminded him that he'd got older and less sure of victory than in the old days. That wasn't necessarily a disadvantage. Even a lion's heart is alone, he mused.

7

John had gone to ground in a castle on the outskirts of Lisieux. Richard gave orders that all avenues of escape from the town were to be sealed off. Anne was part of Richard's retinue. He thought that the meeting with his brother would be trying and that he would need her skills.

He also hoped she would say something that might comfort and encourage him. The words never came.

John's army had diminished considerably after it was learnt that Richard had sailed from Portsmouth. Richard rode through the main street of the town. Everyone he met wanted to betray John. To begin with, the king was amazed, then shocked and, finally, furious.

'It's the king's brother you're denouncing. Have you no shame?' said Richard to an astounded and impecunious peasant who was holding out a cupped hand in the hope of a few coins.

All that the peasant received was a shove. Everyone got out of Richard's way wherever he rode and pointed to the castle on the edge of the town. When he stood before the castle's main gate, ready to attack, they heard the sound of hooves galloping up from behind.

How many were there? He got down on his knees and put his ear to the road.

'There are only five or six,' he said to Anne.

It was a message from Eleanor.

Richard was handed the leather container holding the parchment roll.

Dear Richard, promise me you won't kill him. I've lived long enough to dread the loss of more of my children. If for no other reason, my son, I dare to think that I've had some part in your continued existence. I trust you. As you know, the heart most often remembers its defeats. Those that blacken the bile. While the good memories, those that turn the blood bright red, are of such short duration.

Your devoted mother

Eleanor.

Richard quickly rolled the letter up again.

'Are you there, John?' he shouted.

There was no answer.

Anne was placed in a wagon at the back of Richard's army, with cooks and huntsmen who had the routine responsibility of providing meals. At the very rear came a wagon containing two priests and some deacons who were to attend the dying and dead.

With each word Richard yelled at the main gate, a drowsy lark would rise a few feet above the ground. The mist grew thicker. It fell silent. What was happening? He gave orders to load the crossbows. The portcullis rose. No one was visible inside. Richard ordered the arrows to be lit.

When the gate was open, a figure came into view. He was wearing a blue tunic. The man was bareheaded, close-cropped and clean-shaven. Was there someone behind him? Richard asked those standing nearest if they could recognize him. They shook their heads.

Richard could see that he was barefooted. After a moment three men appeared behind him pushing a hand-cart. They pushed it out in front of their master and tipped out its load, two crossbows, spears, about a hundred bows and quantities of arrows.

'Richard, we surrender!' shouted John.

Richard stared a long time at his brother, his men and, finally, at the top of the fortress, fearing snipers. Did he have any reason to trust him?

'Your men will report to the castle yard and place their weapons in front of the cart. If any one of them doesn't obey, you will all be executed.'

'Great King Richard. We will obey, every one of us!'

Richard rubbed his temples.

One of Richard's men galloped up. 'He's unarmed, Sire. The others have all laid down their weapons.'

'Let him approach.'

John walked towards them.

He fell to his knees in front of Richard. Richard's face showed no signs either of triumph or satisfaction, only revulsion, torment and disgust. John looked Richard in the eye. John's morning aspect spoke of a night filled with horrors and terrible thoughts, Richard mused.

'Mercy.'

Richard drew his sword from its scabbard and turned his back on his brother.

'If you haven't sold yourself to the Devil, you've certainly given him your shadow, John.'

'I'd be the first to understand if you didn't want to forgive me,' John said.

Richard turned to his brother.

'You're a child, John.'

Richard lowered his head and looked at the ground. All went quiet around them.

'You've kept bad company. Others have led you astray,' Richard said. 'They will be punished. Not you. Get up.'

John rose to his feet and tried to embrace his brother. Richard pushed him away.

8

Richard pretended he didn't notice his brother continually looking at him. There was nothing amiss with the food in John's fortress—pheasant, quail, lamb, various fruits, wines, it would have made a victory banquet. Richard ate his fill, got up and walked past Anne.

'What have I done?'

'You've been a bit too generous, perhaps,' she said.

'I've been an over-indulgent fool.'

The tortured face made Anne stretch a hand towards Richard's cheek. She quickly withdrew it.

The victor ambled in to the four-poster bed and lay down on its counterpane. He wished to be alone. Was there anything that could justify his decision to allow his brother to live? What was John good for? He was incompetent on the battlefield and, unquestionably, he was unfit to rule. He couldn't do anything. He always made himself unpopular and showed extremely poor judgement even in the tussle with Richard. He wasn't even a genuine believer. He had no interest in poetry or art.

Richard needed both Hubert and Eleanor in order to overcome Philip. That was the most important thing. If he'd killed John, he would have pleased Hubert, but his mother would never have forgiven him. Wasn't she more important than Walter? The choice was simple. John was in the neighbouring room. Ten soldiers were stationed outside the door. If John were a traitor, what was he himself? His arms and legs were splayed out, like some starfish the waves had smashed against the rocks.

He heard some seagulls outside. Their cries reminded him of human voices. When he was a boy, his mother had said that gulls were executed innocents who'd come back again. That was why God had given them that white plumage. John was no seagull.

Next morning Anne went up to Richard. He stood alone outside the room where they'd eaten breakfast, studying a map of Jerusalem. Anne looked straight at him:

'I've been thinking about something, and I don't know just why I'm asking, but have you actually seen the holy places in Jerusalem?'

Richard studied her face. He saw no trace of malice in it. Could he confide in her?

'Sire, why don't you answer my question? Did you leave Jerusalem without visiting the Church of the Holy Sepulchre?'

'Did I say I hadn't been there?'

Richard didn't know which way to look. He drew breath. 'I've only seen the Holy City from a distance. I need your description of all the things I didn't manage to see. Each night I imagine the city from the Mount of Olives. It lies before me, bathed in golden light.'

Anne left the following morning. She and most of the rest of the retinue were told to return to Anger where Eleanor was in residence.

Richard requested one of his foremost knights, Louis Croix, to listen to his plan: he would take his entire force, which was very well equipped, now that Hubert Walter had supplied the money required, and ride to Philip at Verneuil and take him prisoner. He expected Philip to surrender when he heard he'd been betrayed by John.

Louis Croix thought the plan rather daring and suggested that they divide the army in three and attack one from each side. Croix was sent home. Richard summoned his favourite, William Marshal, and asked him to share the command with him. Richard and Marshal were sure of victory.

Richard rode with Marshal in the vanguard towards Verneuil. The tactics they'd adopted were simple. The army of fifteen thousand men would advance at high speed. The knights and soldiers with lances and slings rode first, the next contingent contained archers who could shoot above the heads of the men in front of them and in the rear came the foot soldiers. They were amazed at how little resistance they encountered.

But, as they quickly realized, they'd made a mistake. Philip's forces had let them advance in order to trap them in a valley. They were attacked on three sides—from the back and from both sides. Richard's men were pointing at Verneuil but not at the enemy. A spear struck Richard unexpectedly from the right and knocked him off his horse.

Marshal got the king to safety behind a hilltop. Richard managed to tell Marshal to take command before he fainted.

When he came to himself, Marshal was standing over him. The wound in his hip wasn't serious. He was aware of a strong smell of blood. Richard passed his hand over his face and throat. His hand was covered in blood. He looked around. Hundreds, perhaps thousands, lay on the ground in contorted postures. Some screamed, others moaned. Most lay still.

'Have we won?' Richard asked.

'It's no victory,' Marshal answered. 'What made you call out "Saladin, save me! Don't let me die here at Ascalon"?'

Richard closed his eyes before turning them towards the wooded hills on either side, the trees, the shadows, the play between the clouds and the beautiful, deep blue sky. Not one but innumerable thoughts came, they were like grains of sand drifting into a ridge that hid everything that was lovely and good. Couldn't he wield his sword with the same power as he used to? Was he thinking too much? Was that what Saladin had found out? There it was again, that troublesome thought, that Saladin was simply a human being, created by God, in God's image, someone for whom God had had a purpose.

Close by him someone screamed. A blinded soldier had risen and tripped over a dead horse.

Richard could see that the man lying next to him hadn't long to live. His hair was long and matted, the knife was still in his belly.

'Haven't I seen you before?' whispered the man.

'I don't think so,' Richard answered.

'Will you promise to say to my wife that I ask her forgiveness for joining in this meaningless war? She was against it. But we needed the money. Tell her I died a believer.'

'What's her name?'

'Sara Breton.'

Richard looked away before turning to the man again, nodding slowly.

Philip managed to hold the remnants of his force together and established new headquarters half a day's march from Verneuil. Richard realized that he must strengthen his army and withdrew his soldiers. And that wasn't all. He also had to initiate closer diplomatic cooperation with Navarre, Toulouse and Flanders. Over the years he'd become a wilier and less irascible negotiator, if he understood himself correctly. His marriage to Berengaria was fundamental to his good relations with Navarre and King Sancho, her brother. Were his talks successful, Toulouse and Flanders would certainly join Sancho and him in a combined force against Philip. The fact that Philip was losing would probably make them biddable. He summoned his two best horsemen and ordered them to ride as fast as possible to King Sancho at Pamplona. Richard's letter to his brother-in-law didn't stand on ceremony.

> *Dear Sancho, king of Navarre and brother. The hour of destiny is upon us. The closeness between our two royal houses has never been stronger. If, together, we crush Philip and his army, our realms will become larger and more powerful. We have managed to inflict much damage on him.*

Then he sent messengers to the courts of Flanders and Toulouse. Sancho's answer was immediate and positive. The other two replied guardedly. Four weeks later, Navarre's army attacked Philip's forces. Richard fell on him from the other side. At Fréteval, Richard gave orders to take Philip alive.

Yet again Philip managed to get away. But not his baggage train and a large part of his court. The spoils included a large amount of gold and silver coin, horses, soldiers, dressers, cooks, servants, gems, gold, regalia, the royal archives and several years' worth of intelligence material. This wasn't enough to mollify Richard's fury that Philip had evaporated.

William Marshal tried to soothe Richard by telling him that just outside Angoulême, 'by the grace of God', they'd managed to take three hundred knights and forty thousand soldiers.

'I don't want to hear any excuses. Ten times the amount of gold and prisoners couldn't make up for this. It's a disaster that you,' said Richard, pointing to Marshal, Robert of Thornham and Geoffrey de la Celle, 'didn't manage to take him. We control everything from Scotland to the Pyrenees but we can't get hold of the towns of Rouen, Caen and Falaise in Normandy.'

The stalemate between Richard's and Philip's forces was so entrenched that when Thornham jokingly suggested that the war could be settled by a five-a-side duel, Richard said it was a good idea. Philip and he should be one of the five, he thought.

He would have won ninety-nine out of a hundred duels. But what if he slipped, not noticed a wet, yellowing leaf on the ground and fallen? It would be typical of Philip's luck, to be helped by a dead leaf.

The great bird circled. Was it an eagle? No, it was completely black. When Richard rode nearer, he recognized it as a raven. He was on his way to see Sara Breton near Tours. He dreaded imparting the news of her husband's death. The raven flew silently making several gliding circles before it decided to sail along the adjacent hillside. There were few weather omens Richard had so much faith in as the one that claimed that a raven flying high would bring rain. If it had flown low and croaked, it would have meant fine weather.

Richard set his horse to a gallop, black clouds were coming from the east, he wanted to get under cover before the sky opened. He wore a long, plain blue cloak with a hood. Round his waist was a belt that carried his sword. He wanted to meet the widow without too much fuss. An elderly grey-haired man was standing outside a hovel. The weather was cold. The man was barefooted. Richard asked where Sara lived. The man pointed and said that she was waiting for her husband and the money for his war service.

Sara lived in a shack of what Richard assumed was driftwood from the nearby river, mixed with branches and clay. It was in a huddle of other shacks. A blanket served as a door. Richard wouldn't have been happy if the pigs or the wild boars at the castle had been housed like this. What strange smells assailed him, even though the blanket was pulled across the door. He heard the crying of children. He tried to rehearse what he had to say. The words wouldn't come. Richard realized that he hadn't a single coin on him.

The blanket was pulled aside. He recognized her immediately. She'd got thinner, her face was brown, whether from dirt or from the sun he didn't know. She studied him, came a couple of paces closer. He wondered if he should jump down from his horse and introduce himself. She came right up to the horse and patted it. Four children appeared. The eldest, a boy of barely ten, was carrying a baby. It was sniffling. People poured out of the huts round about. He counted more than forty, of all ages. He felt himself tensing. He reached quickly for his sword, he felt as he had in the market at Jericho. They were just like the Saracens who had surrounded him then; the eyes, the wavering smiles, the dirty faces, the rags they wore. What was the difference between these people in front of him and those of Jericho?

He looked at Sara and let go of the hilt.

'I must talk to you alone,' Richard said.

He saw her prominent cheekbones beneath her head covering, her mouth and her large, light-blue eyes above the grey, worn shift.

She put her hand to her forehead. He didn't know why. She opened her eyes again, shooed the children inside and told her neighbours to go about their own business.

'Perhaps your children would like to sit on my horse,' Richard whispered.

'Don't get off your horse, Your Majesty. Your face tells me why you're here. Don't say it. Or they'll have . . .' she nodded in the direction of her children before continuing, '... no hope left.'

Richard swallowed. He tugged off his ring and gave it her. He was relieved that she took it.

'Thank you,' he said. 'Please melt it down.'

Sara turned and went in. She pulled the blanket across without a single word.

Richard rode towards Brittany to prepare the next attack on Philip's forces. On his way to the coast, not far from Lorient where, he reckoned, Philip had his headquarters, his mind wandered back to one of his first meetings with Philip and his sister Alys in Paris. Certainly, Alys had been beautiful, but Philip was far more interesting. Alys quickly realized that Richard would rather spend his time on her brother and said she hadn't time to keep them company. Philip wasn't good-looking, not even then, not at all, but inquisitive, attentive and very young. At first Richard had been irritated by how admiring and obsequious he was. It was obvious he was eight years younger. But Richard was impressed by the way he wanted to learn all the things he wasn't good at, like using a lance, speaking verse and swimming. And something that impressed Richard from the first moment was that he possessed a natural 'regal authority'. He *knew* he would be king, he didn't boast about it, rather, he would lower his voice if the subject arose. Richard loved Paris from the first moment he saw the city. Philip and he had wandered side by side, street after street, the isles in the Seine—Île de la Cité and Île

Saint-Louis. Philip had pointed out and spoken of Notre Dame, the cloisters, the royal castle, they'd strolled in parks, they'd laughed, they'd walked across to the Right Bank, to La Ville, seen the sailmakers and coopers at work, walked along the Left Bank, ambled through the harbour of Saint-Germain, studied the university, looked out from Rue de la Huchette, the hospital, the great Hôtel Dieu which lay right down on the waterfront, played bowls and become more and more intimate. He was so humble and shy, but also playful, he flirted and teased in a manner that had gratified Richard. In fact, he loved it. They'd enjoyed an untroubled summer together in Paris, when they'd been alone, without titles or courts or realms making demands of them. Richard smiled as he recollected how irritated it had made Philip when he'd used his full name —Philip Augustus. He'd gone on saying Augustus in a mocking tone, as if he'd been named after Emperor Augustus or, even worse, Caesar's horse, until they'd had a mock fight beneath the ancient, shady maples.

And now, Richard thought, all his thoughts were taken up with only one thing—how he could kill him. The will to destroy him was all the greater because the memories were so good. He wanted to avenge his treachery.

After the battle, Richard received a letter from Eleanor. He trembled as he read it. He felt his eyes filling.

Dear Richard,

I am ill. Some might call it serious. I would like to see you so much. Life doesn't last for ever.

Richard instructed Marshal to take command and, that same evening, rode to Anger as fast as he could. Breathless, he rushed into the castle and towards his mother's private apartments. He was expecting to find her in the big four-poster bed. The bed and the room were empty. Had he arrived too late? He made for where the chamberlains ate and apportioned their daily tasks.

He ran into her half way down the passage.

'I heard that you'd come.'

'But aren't you seriously ill?'

'So you only want to visit me when I'm dying? I haven't seen you for months. I had to write that to get you here.'

'I'm in the middle of a war.'

'It looks as if you're not going to defeat Philip either, Richard. Shall we make an alliance with another country to defeat Philip once and for all?'

'Do you think I can't do it without help?'

'You've already used Sancho and Navarre. We must get a stronger ally. Your time in the Holy Land has depleted you more than I thought. You won't have me for ever.'

She looked down at the floor. It was a long time since Richard had seen his mother so thoughtful.

'Life is a ridiculous and painful battle against inevitable collapse. Age makes you neither wiser nor kinder. And your sight, hearing and back don't improve, my son. But I'm against death. It's meaningless.'

'But, Mother, what's the matter with you?'

'There's meaning to the tribulations of age. But that wasn't all I wanted to say. I'm having a present made for you.'

'It's not the time for presents,' Richard said and sprinted out of the castle and mounted his horse.

He patted it and asked himself if he'd become too old to lead the war against Philip. Was he in the process of forgetting that he was God's chosen one? He peered down his torso. Although his cloak hid much, it was easy to see that he wasn't as fit as he'd been. His mother and Hubert would certainly have discussed the fact, that God's sword was no longer as wieldy as it once had been. They would learn that he could strike a blow. Hard and merciless.

Anne was mulching herbs in the winter garden as Richard came riding towards her. He hadn't seen her for a long time. He reined in his horse by a pear tree. He looked at her. She didn't appear to have noticed him. She continued spreading pine twigs and straw round the delicate plants. Quite suddenly she turned to him and said with fury in her voice:

'You ordered your forces to fight Philip on Good Friday. What is the matter with you?'

'This is a war I *have* to win.'

9

For several months Richard had been overseeing the building of his gigantic castle and palace, Château Gaillard, on the island of Les Andelys in the Seine. It was to be his future residence and fortress. The fortress occupied a particularly favourable strategic position. It was one day's march from Philip's main seat at Gaillon and Paris was only half a day's journey up the Seine.

Richard summoned Anne.

When her carriage drew up in the castle yard, Richard was busy inspecting the work of three bricklayers on the other side of the fortress. The bricklayers threw trowels of mortar from a bucket on to the stones, which were carefully placed one above the other. After the first throw they tapped the remainder of the mortar into the bucket before using the trowel to remove what was squeezing out between the square stones. With their left hand they carefully tested the stone to make sure it was seated firmly before lifting another stone and repeating all the well-rehearsed movements. Anne was standing in the castle yard shading her eyes. She waved to him.

Richard was keen to show her round.

The walls were designed so that there would be no blind spot when defending the castle, Richard explained, and added that it would be the world's finest fortress. While he spoke he climbed a ladder that was leaning against the wall to show her how cleverly the loopholes had been shaped.

'Why are you going up there without mail on? You might be hit by someone in Philip's service,' Anne called. 'And now you're openly standing on top of the wall without protection?'

Richard descended the ladder with some difficulty, going up was easier on his knee. He stood by her side.

'This fortress is costing me more than all my other fortresses and castles in England put together. Château Gaillard isn't merely a bulwark against Rouen but also an important base for conquering Vexin. Isn't it beautiful? It's a wonderful view, admit it. There's the sea and there the Seine, almost all the way to Paris.'

She nodded and smiled.

'I need your advice, Anne. That's why I sent for you. Something ominous has happened. I'm at odds with the bishop of Rouen. He maintains that I've no right to build here.'

'What happened?'

'The sun went dark in the middle of the day. A shower of blood fell from the sky and besmirched the unfinished walls. I believe it was *me* God was talking to,' Richard said.

'I don't necessarily think it was caused by the bishop. He might have something else He wanted to say to you?'

'Oh?' said Richard relieved.

'Maybe He's blaming you for not killing the Antichrist.'

Richard turned away. The words cut him worse than the slash of a sword.

He heard the wind in the loopholes above them and the flapping of the pennants.

He looked out through an opening in the wall—broadleaved trees, bracken, but also an alley of poplars. It was autumn. A flock of birds in *v*-formation flew rapidly towards the south.

'What I don't understand,' said Anne, 'is why now, several years after Saladin's death, you neither take Jerusalem nor visit the city but spend all your energy in a war with Philip.'

'I came so close to defeating Saladin. But even after his death, he's able to make me realize that I lost. I'm plagued with heretical thoughts. I'm not sure if Saladin wasn't more faithful to the code of chivalry than most knights are. Don't you see that I'm in the process of becoming his eternal hostage?'

10

It started to snow. First came fat, wet snowflakes. Then flurries of lighter flakes. Just before they touched the ground, they began to rise again. Richard was inspecting the building work on the northern tower.

A fanfare rolled through the air. His mother and Walter were expected. He hurried up the flights of steps within the fortress so that he could see them turn into the castle yard. He ran faster than was good for his knee. It had been almost two years since he'd last seen Walter. His mother was the same.

Walter had visibly aged and thinned. Richard could see that his shiny pate was ringed with grey hair. Since their last meeting contact between them had been restricted to letters and messengers. Richard had not missed him. He assumed the feeling was mutual. Richard enjoyed observing him from above. He looked even smaller. Did the building actually impress him a little? Should he shout to him? No, he wanted to look at him a bit longer. Hubert said something to his travelling companions, who took the baggage and disappeared. He went over to the wall and stroked the sand-hued stone with his fingers. Hubert had often said that the fortress at Kerak, east of the Dead Sea, was the mightiest construction he'd ever seen. Was he about to change his mind? There was no doubting that Hubert administered England and Richard's interests in the British Isles well. Richard was pleased he could forego crossing the Channel. He could have wished for more control over Hubert's activities. But, provided he didn't hinder his war with Philip, Richard had no desire to oust him. And, surely, the sight of Château Gaillard must bring him to the realization that the fortress wasn't only impregnable, it was a bridgehead to the conquest of territory to the east—not just the Countship of Vexin but also Burgundy, Flanders, Lorraine, Provence, Paris and right across to the Holy Roman Empire.

Richard hailed them. The wind whisked away his words. They were helped inside by various servants.

When he met them in the hall, they were sitting in muted conversation.

'It's good to see you all. Especially you, Hubert, after your hazardous Channel crossing. It's been a long time,' said Richard.

'I think I'll leave you gentlemen now. I can hear by my son's tone that he wants to have a man-to-man talk. We'll speak at dinner.'

She beckoned her two servants. With a little help she managed to get out of the high-backed chair and disappeared.

'Château Gaillard is every bit as impressive as rumour suggests,' said Hubert.

'That wasn't why you came.'

There was a slight pause.

'Is it about the costs of the war with Philip, or the price of Château Gaillard?'

'I was surprised that you didn't kill John. You listened to your mother, I presume.'

'You don't miss me in England, Hubert?'

'Even in old England we hear of your feats on the battlefield. The last I heard from the messenger was that Philip only just managed to reach the safety of the castle at Gisors. Is it true that you were so close to capturing him that twenty of his household troops drowned in the moat? Is that the third or the fourth time he's slipped through your fingers?'

'Have you come here to taunt me?'

'You've been unlucky. You know quite well that I've supported you through what we may surely, er, term this *lengthy* war with Philip. It's only a year since I got you fifty knights and five thousand men.'

'What were you and my mother talking about?'

'I've had a meeting with the papal envoy, Peter of Capua. The pope wants the war between you and Philip to cease. He wants you to be reconciled and to begin a new Crusade.'

'What's your opinion, Hubert?'

Walter was silent.

'You're making the pope's envoy say what *you* want, aren't you?'

'You're the undisputed leader, Richard. You'll have the first pick of the territories in the Holy Land.'

'Don't you understand that it's impossible for Philip and me to work together. Last time it took him almost four years to get started. D'you want to squeeze the life out of me down there in the heat?'

'How much land have you managed to take in the war with Philip?'

Richard was breathing deeply. Surely Hubert must see how angry he was? Had he got his mother to side with him? Richard was ashamed of the thought. Naturally she would never have supported anything of the sort, certainly not unless the two of them had talked it over first. Never.

'Capua, the papal envoy, suggests a five-year peace accord. And that Philip's son marries one of your nieces. Possibly the daughter of the king of Castile might be suitable?'

Richard stared at the man before him. Hubert was thin, with clean-cut features and a well-trimmed beard and moustache. Around one narrow, hirsute wrist hung a thin silver chain. He was normally polite, never loud-spoken, didn't gesticulate, but produced his carefully measured sentences with a meekness that gave the impression that he was frightened they might break if anyone raised a voice in his presence.

Richard mused that if he pulled the little man out of his chair and throttled him, he would barely be able to make a sound.

He rose, said something to Walter about needing fresh air and went out on to the balcony. Walter remained seated. Richard scanned the Seine. He closed his eyes. What he saw was blue sea, with countless blue waves, like the sea off Acre.

'Now will you tell me what else is on your mind?' Richard asked with as much control as he could muster when he came back in.

'Does this nun have an especially good influence on you?'

Walter sat fiddling with the chain round his wrist.

'Eleanor is impressed with Anne Hofer. By the way, don't try and curry favour with my mother. She supports my battle to win the whole of France, as she did previously. We'll be mortal enemies if you try to split us. D'you hear me?'

'Sire, I would never do that. Truly, the world has rarely seen a better or closer bond between a mother and son.'

Was Hubert being sarcastic? No other person could make Richard feel so insecure.

He was silent. Hubert went on:

'Did you know that a certain Jacques Breton has applied to your mother?'

'What did Breton want?'

'To warn you that thousands of peasants are planning a revolt against the war because they can't grow their crops. They're dying of hunger.'

'I know what's being grown.'

'Breton said that the number of farm animals has more than halved. The peasants need work. They miss the Crusade.'

A servant knocked at the door. The two looked at each other. From the far side of the door came the announcement: 'Dinner is served, Sire.'

'I won't have any,' Richard shouted.

Hubert Walter got up, bowed and went out.

Richard sat staring at the wall. The body, he mused, is principally a container for the heart. God grants the heart an allotted span before halting it and giving the key to the angel of the resurrection.

The door swung ajar. Richard got up to shut it. As he did so he saw Anne standing with Hubert on the stairs leading down to the dining hall. Hubert was speaking, Anne nodding. Richard disliked the sight. Just as he saw Hubert begin to turn in his direction, Richard called the nun to him.

She came running up the stairs. Richard closed the door behind her.

'Aren't you eating?' Anne asked. 'Walter told me you'd had a pleasant conversation.'

'What else did he tell you?'

'That the pope wants you to lead another Crusade. You're made for it, Richard.'

'Did he ask you to say that?'

She looked at him uncertainly. 'But it's true.'

Richard slapped her face. She fell forwards. He left her lying there. Anne gazed up at him. She tried to rise, steadying herself on the edge of the table, she grasped Richard's cloak and hauled herself up. She took a step back and stood there looking at him. He began to pace to and fro, sending her a furtive glance now and again.

'Go,' he said.

11

All the guests at Château Gaillard had been invited to a
concert. Richard refused to go. Through a servant he asked
Anne for a detailed account. She promised to do this as
conscientiously as possible. She had hardly been outside
her room during the past week because of the bruise on her
cheek. She was looking forward to it. The concert was to
begin just before midnight. She stood high on the battle-
ment looking out across the sea. The moon was partially
obscured by clouds that drifted across the sky.

There weren't more than twenty in the audience. The
concert took place in one of the smaller halls. The thick
walls made it cool and pleasant. Torches burnt along the
passage leading to the hall. In the chamber, candles on two
large tables flickered in the draught from the open door.
The door was closed. A woman appeared before the audience. Anne didn't recognize her.

There was complete silence as the woman, visibly
nervous, cleared her throat and tugged at her silver neck-
lace with its gold cross pendant studded with diamonds.
From the chair behind her Anne could hear Hubert Walter's voice whispering: 'Presumably this is the last time
we'll hear her limited repertoire.' He was sitting next to
Eleanor.

The other listeners clearly knew who the fleshy singer was. As soon as Anne could make out the words, she knew it as well. It was Richard's wife, Queen Berengaria. After a few introductory songs she attempted to reach a vocal climax, without success. Her raven-black locks fell to her shoulders. She clasped the brooch beneath her bosom and received the sedentary, civil applause as if it were a standing ovation.

The morning after the concert Anne asked one of Richard's chamberlains how he was.

'He's in his rooms and doesn't want to be disturbed.'

She went out into the courtyard where her carriage had drawn up when she'd arrived at Château Gaillard a few days earlier. Now, a far larger one stood ready for departure. Eight horses were attached to the closed carriage which had Richard's arms emblazoned on its door. Behind it were two smaller wagons for clothes chests which servants were stowing. Each of these wagons had four horses. Who was leaving? Surely not Richard already? She hastened to the carriage. He mustn't leave without speaking to her. She opened the door. The rider of a nearby horse shouted something she didn't hear. The inside of the carriage was in semi-darkness. Two people occupied it. They said nothing. They resembled one another. Their skins were darker than Anne's. One was a lady-in-waiting, the other Queen Berengaria of England.

'Are you the only one to wish us farewell?' said the queen.

'Farewell?' Anne repeated hesitantly.

'I'm being sent home to Navarre. I was told of it just before the concert. The pope, Hubert Walter and my husband all think that the alliance between England and Navarre must cease. I have no use any more.'

Anne turned and glanced across the empty yard.

'The worst thing is that no one loves him except me. He never worried that we were childless. His member was only stiff when he went to war.'

'Gracious madam, she's a nun,' exclaimed the lady-in-waiting.

'Forgive me.'

The carriage began to move. Anne only just managed to jump off the step without falling.

12

'The Archbishop of Canterbury, Hubert Walter!' called the guard.

Richard was bent over his writing table making a list of deficiencies in the fortress which he wanted to discuss with the master mason later that day.

'Show him in.'

'Your Majesty.'

Richard studied the document before him.

'Why so formal, Hubert? Thank you for sending Berengaria home.'

Richard looked up. 'Today I want to ask you to accompany Eleanor to Anjou before returning to England yourself. I need you there.'

'But I thought . . .'

'Thank you, that's all. Show him out.'

Anne was summoned.

She was dressed in a long, turquoise silk gown, a gold chain around her neck. Her hair wasn't plaited, but fell loose to her shoulders.

Richard turned and stared out of the window in the direction of Rouen Cathedral.

'I haven't seen your hair like that before,' he said, turning to face her.

She was carrying a basket of ointments for rubbing into his temples, forehead and throat, to get rid of headaches.

She told of the concert and of her meeting with Berengaria in the castle yard.

'There is something I must tell you after your treatment.'

'Can't you tell me now?'

'No, it would distract you. The ointments are supposed to be calming.'

'So the thing you want to tell me will be disquieting?'

'I've said too much, obviously.'

'Speak up. I thought you'd come to ease my headache?'

'It's about Queen Eleanor and Hubert Walter. They were sitting behind me at the concert. Because the queen was having difficulty hearing, Walter whispered just loud enough for me to hear. Walter had learnt from the papal envoy that you're to be canonized. I'm so proud on your behalf.'

'You know that I don't deserve it. Can I be frank with you?'

'Yes,' said Anne, nodding eagerly.

'I feel rather . . .'

Richard fell silent.

'Alone. Is that what you mean?' asked Anne.

He nodded.

'The convent has told me they're still waiting for the money. Is there something I'm not doing right? I don't want to disappoint you or my sisters.'

'I'm sorry. I'll look into it.'

'Would you take your upper garments off? I'll apply a herbal mixture that will do you good.'

He obeyed.

She rubbed the mixture in, using two fingers of one hand. She took pains over his temples and brow. Richard noticed that she hesitated momentarily before massaging the ointment into his chest with the palm of her hand.

'Can I do anything more for you, Richard?'

'Tell me about the Holy City.'

Anne spoke of the olive trees in Jerusalem, of the eucalyptuses, palms, poppies, fig trees, anemones, jasmines, gladioli, narcissi, the plane trees with their trunks and leaves. And of the scarlet, pink and orange flowers of the hibiscus, of how its leaves turned an ever-deeper green.

He closed his eyes.

He could hear that she was breathing more rapidly.

He opened his eyes. His headache was gone. She looked as if she were hot, she was staring at him, why wasn't she massaging any more? Suddenly she went quite still. She raised her arms and pulled her gown over her head. She was naked. She said that she'd never been naked in front of any man. A breeze stroked her white body. The turquoise garment lay like a garland at her feet. He said nothing at first. They held each other's gaze.

He could see that she had a beautiful body. Her dark-red nipples pointed straight ahead.

He'd never felt such pleasure in talking to anyone as her. Her person and soul had attracted him. He turned his face away.

'I can't, I won't,' he said.

'I thought . . .'

'What did you think?'

'That you had to have me before the convent got its money.'

13

'You've obviously spent the night in that chair.'

It was his mother who woke him.

Wolf II lay next to Richard. Eleanor's voice caused the dog to open one eye. He stretched his great, grey-haired body, yawned and fell asleep again.

'You've changed so much recently, Richard.'

'You didn't knock. What do you want?'

'Even though you banished me some days ago, I'm tough enough to return without an invitation.'

'I've got the impression that you and Hubert are laying plans for my future behind my back. Why did you and Hubert pay my ransom?'

'You are my favourite child.'

'At least you and I ought to stick together in this mad world. There aren't many men who've admired their mothers more than I have, you know that.'

'Isn't it strange, Richard, how childhood becomes lovelier with time, a forgotten journey one can invest with whatever one likes. That's how it is for me, anyway,' said Eleanor.

'I find people hard to understand.'

'I never even understood my husbands. And you children, you're all so different. Although I think I've nearly always understood you.'

Richard turned his gaze to the window and looked out.

'It's only recently that I've become unsure of you. You're the person closest to me. You know what he's like, he doesn't say it, but it's more and more obvious that he's against the war with Philip. Did you know that? Have you got confidence in me? You understand that Philip must be beaten before there can be any talk of a new Crusade to Jerusalem? Fighting wars is hard, Mother. If my nearest and dearest aren't with me, it's impossible.'

Eleanor patted his hair: 'Haven't I always supported you?'

At the same moment, in Venice, Doge Enrico Dandolo called a meeting of the City Council. In collaboration with the pope he wished to equip a fourth Crusade to drive off Saladin's successors. The pope had lost faith in Richard's ability to lead a new Crusade. The doge put forward a plan for plundering Constantinople on the way to Jerusalem. Three quarters of all the gold in the world went through Constantinople. The world's biggest church, Hagia Sofia, together with twenty-four other churches in the city, contained more than twice as much gold and precious stones as Ravenna and Venice combined. If one included the riches of the emperor's palace, it would surpass the value of Rome and Beijing. In addition, Constantinople had the world's finest library and university.

That same afternoon the bookseller in St Mark's Square, Procuratie Vécchie, was ordered to run off maps of the capital of the Byzantine Empire.

14

Richard was eating nettle soup from an earthenware bowl when Anne entered the room. He had hoped she'd gone. She was dressed in a long, dark-red woollen dress. Her throat was bare. He got up and looked out. The sky was peach-coloured and downy with sun. They were opposite one another when Richard began to speak. The sentences were short. The words were awkward and tumbled out. Anne grasped his wrist. Her grip was like a warm ring. Even now, he thought, I can feel my heart beating and the bones and joints moving inside me.

'Sister Anne, I must ask you to go tomorrow.'

'Where?'

'To your convent.'

'Is that your own wish?'

'You'll get a larger lump sum for your convent.'

'Thank you,' she said, and gave the bowl on the table a shove.

The hot soup spilt between his thighs.

Richard bent over quickly.

She halted at the door. He tried to straighten up. He drew a deep breath. She turned towards him.

'I'm going off to pack. But there's one last thing I want to say—you've helped the lie about your conquest of

Jerusalem to take root because you've never told your people the truth. And also, you realize now that you'll never be able to regain the Holy City, even if you kill Philip and take the whole of France. That's the truth, isn't it? Isn't it?' she shouted and ran off.

Richard quickly removed his hose and looked at the burn. It was painful, but not extensive. When she returned to her convent, she would doubtless unburden herself to the prioress, give her the money, relate how lust had flared up and made her tear her clothes off. And just as certainly, the prioress wouldn't speak of sin and punishment but would ask Anne to repeat what had happened while she closed her eyes and sighed.

'Depraved beggars,' Richard shouted.

By the side of the upset bowl lay the parchment signed by Hubert Walter. Richard satisfied himself that he was alone and then read the two final sentences out loud:

My Lord, your mother, the pope and I advise, most earnestly, that you ride at the head of a new Holy Army against Jerusalem. We require your signature.

Richard wasn't in any doubt. Hubert Walter had betrayed him. Behind his back his foremost servant, whose sole and overriding duty was to obey the king's command, had begun to operate on his own behalf. Did Hubert Walter imagine that he, the King of England, would tolerate his servant's game? Had he completely lost all sense of judgement? This would be his downfall. Walter would suffer for his insolence in pretending he had Richard's mother with him in this intrigue.

Who knew her best? Hubert Walter or him? Richard sat down, got up. There is nothing more silent than a crushed heart, but is there anything noisier than a pompous, overbearing and conceited one? Such was Walter's. Richard paced round the table. He propped himself against the wall on outstretched arms, talked to himself, saw Walter's face in his mind's eye, studied the wall and seated himself. Did Walter imagine that from now on he could control his mother and him? How much had Walter received from the pope for selling him to the next Crusade? Was Walter, in whom he'd placed the greatest confidence and trust, whether in personal matters or those of state, in the process of exchanging his intellectual wisdom for folly and greed?

Richard got up, gripping the table, kicked the chair, which almost fell over. He splayed his fingers and pressed the tips into the table. He bent his body forward. It was painful. His middle fingers were on the point of breaking when he lifted his head and stared up at the beams in the ceiling. He straightened up and removed his hands.

Was he becoming frightened of Walter's oily, metallic gaze, his calculating words which always contained at least one ulterior motive, his brilliant hypocrisy and his formulations which were consciously fashioned not to be too precise? If these qualities, which previously had served his interests, were now turned *against* him, what should he do to counter him?

Richard tore up the parchment, went out of the door with purposeful strides and called for servants and the castle's officer of the watch.

He told them that he would take two regiments that evening and ride towards Châlus-Chabrol, the castle of Philip's vassal. Only a tiny force had to be overcome. Twenty-eight men had weapons, ten had hammers and spades and kitchen utensils. A couple only had their fists. Richard had ten times as many men. Heavily armed. Several of his commanders asked why he didn't delegate the job to them. Surely he had better things to do? Richard made no answer.

They besieged the castle for three days, so as not to destroy the beautiful building.

The forty men inside Châlus-Chabrol were on the point of surrender. From the walls, a man hurled a stone at Richard. Richard leapt aside, picked up the stone and threw it back. The man defended himself with a frying pan. Richard laughed and ambled off to his tent to search for a map he couldn't find. When he returned, the man with the frying pan was still there. It was only now that Richard saw how young he was. Maybe fifteen? He shouted abuse at the king and laughed at him. The king went off to eat.

Richard had two chicken legs and then left his tent to see how things were developing. He stretched and felt his knee.

'Put on your mail, Sire. We don't know when they'll start using more serious weapons,' shouted Richard's officer-in-command.

The youth with the frying pan chucked a kitchen knife at Richard. Richard clapped his hands and laughed out loud, as if it were a game, while the knife was still in the air. Richard ducked too late and received the knife in his left shoulder. He turned away so that no one would see what had happened. He didn't call out or tell anyone that he'd been injured. He walked slowly back to his tent. The knife was still embedded in his arm. Just inside the flap he groaned. He tried to pull it out. The handle broke off. The blade remained.

Within the hour the castle was taken without the destruction of anything valuable. But where was the king? The men assumed he was sleeping in his tent. When they found him, the blade was removed and the wound cleansed. He was carried into the castle. The wound turned gangrenous.

15

Richard lay in the castle's biggest bed. He was shivery and feverish by turns. Eleanor and Hubert Walter arrived at his sickbed two days after he'd been wounded. Even though one is dying, one isn't dead, Richard thought. It is faith that causes one to lower one's eyes, so that death can take charge, so that one expires peacefully in the shadow of one's eyelids, instead of dying like some foolish colossus with straining muscles who believes he can conquer the unconquerable. A white light filled the room.

Saladin sat by Richard's side.

'You're dead, aren't you?' Richard asked.

Saladin nodded. He was even thinner than Richard had imagined. His skin was yellow.

'Death was a peaceful experience. Three of my grandchildren were playing bowls on the grass in front of me. I was sitting beneath an olive tree in the park in Damascus and my friend Behaeddin was talking to me.'

'That must have been pleasant.'

'It was indeed. But Richard, why did you attack Jerusalem with just your household troops and not your *entire* force?'

'My advisers said that if we'd managed to take the city, we'd have had considerable problems holding Jerusalem because of the long supply lines to the coast.'

'You would have destroyed all the holy places, all the churches, mosques, synagogues and the Via Dolorosa. It's possible that you would have succeeded with the help of Greek fire.'

'That fire gives us great power.'

'If you had destroyed the whole city and massacred all the Muslims, Jews and Christians who were against you, a new leader would have been born to my people, they would have risen again and again.'

'Were you certain of that?'

'Not entirely.'

'Isn't it strange how so many victories are built on ignorance and self-confidence, Saladin?'

'And what is a victory really? Under the walls of Acre, after you had gained the "victory", I saw you murder in the basest manner. And yet I recognized something in you. Something that was part of me. During the battle of Hattin eleven years ago, when we finally managed to crush you, I wallowed in gore, I thrust, I hacked, I thirsted for revenge. I felt a little as I did when we conquered the Shias in Egypt.'

'So you weren't only noble?'

'When you thought you'd killed everyone, Richard, when no one screamed, when all was still, when you and your men went among the corpses and the dying and drove your swords into those who were still breathing, you lost everything. Your face and hair were full of blood.

You were a vulture that had raised its head from carrion. But vultures leave off when they are sated. You were insatiable.'

'Be quiet. You have killed innocents as well. What was the name of that poet and Sufi? Yahia al-Suhrawardi?'

'At Hattin I was like you. Revenge was sweet at first, then it turned to poison. When I took Jerusalem, "revenge" was the cry that went up from my officers, I refused, not because I'm noble but because I knew I would gain greater personal contentment that way. If I had destroyed the city and avenged myself, it would have provoked even greater revenge from you.'

'My mother and Hubert Walter want to do all they can to idolize me after my death, you know. They've both realized they'll profit by it.'

'Richard, my uneasiness stems from the way my fellow believers place more emphasis on the victory over the Crusaders at the battle of Hattin than on my peaceful conquest of Jerusalem.'

'Why did you spare me at Ascalon, Saladin?'

'Don't you think that your Christian brothers will remember our good deeds at Ascalon and Jerusalem for all time?'

Richard caught the scent of lavender.

'Why are you talking about that Saracen in your sleep, Richard?'

It was Eleanor speaking. He tried to sit up but fell back, exhausted.

He looked straight at her. This was his mother. Even now, despite the pain, the blurred vision and the vomiting, he recognized her outline, whereas his surroundings grew ever more indistinct. The smells and sounds of the room were at one moment easy to recognize before vanishing the next. It almost seemed as if smell and sound were becoming less and less important to him. He gazed round the room several times. Each time it was the same. It only lodged in his mind once he'd managed to single out his mother. It had always been like this. Mother, son, son, mother. Sun and moon, sky and sea. She raised her hand, then dropped it as if not knowing what to do with her thin, bony fingers. Her mouth twitched. She glanced furtively at Walter, at the servants, the ring on her finger, made of gold and amber, started to say something, left it hanging, looked at him with a look as if she weren't sure whether he heard or understood what she'd said. It was his mother who wanted to witness the farewell, the cessation of all his qualities and characteristics—the son, the swimmer, God's Sword, king, Crusader, John's brother and Philip's arch-enemy, she stood at his bedside to see all this life turn to memories.

She had great difficulty walking to and fro at the foot of the bed. Very rarely did she accept the offer of a seat. She was mumbling. Was she mumbling to Hubert? Were they exchanging glances? It didn't look like it. She clamped the hand, which had so recently been redundant, round the silver mounting of her stick. Her eyes were unnaturally large.

Richard grasped the servant who stood next to him and tried to haul himself up into a sitting position. Only a few indecipherable words came after several long, heavy gasps. His legs were impossible to lift, some of his toes curled, his knees bent a fraction, his elbow obeyed him, he felt that a muscle in his upper arm was on his side. But there wasn't anything wrong with his head. It was there, between his ears. He became uneasy watching his mother's suffering eyes, or were they merely pensive? Nearly everyone is tough enough to bear the pain of others. His mother looked to be one of them.

'Richard, you said there was something you wanted to confess?'

He thought for a long time.

'Did I say that? Now I remember—I would have plunged a knife lustily into John and Philip without any regret. But as for Saladin . . .'

He struggled for breath. '. . . I couldn't have done it.'

'Speak softer,' she whispered. 'That blue silk night-gown suits you, Richard,' she said loudly. 'You have brought the Cross of Jesus back to the faithful and given us the chance to see the Holy City.'

'It's not true, Mother. Saladin gave it to us when he took Jerusalem. We lost territory, support and all the chivalrous virtues you taught me.'

'You're having nightmares. You're hot and sweating.'

Richard dozed.

'I've only got you and John left. I don't deserve to see you lying . . . like this. Have I told you about the present I'm going to give you, Richard? You've been to Bayeux Cathedral and seen the tapestry that's more than two hundred feet long? It's marvellous to see how the Norman victory at the battle of Hastings is portrayed. Remember all the people and soldiers and animals on the tapestry?'

'Mother, I'm tired. I don't deserve anything.'

'I've had a tapestry made that's even bigger than the one at Bayeux. You should have had it on your fortieth birthday, but the weavers and sempsters weren't finished.'

'And so you have to speak of this surprise because you know that I'll never see it with my own eyes?'

'Three hundred people weaving and sewing day and night, it will be ready in a couple of weeks. They've been working on it for two years.'

He didn't know why but he enjoyed seeing her so unable to cope with the situation that she couldn't reply. Should he tell her? Why was he so hard on her? Weren't they both frightened of losing their regal pomp and just becoming ordinary people dissolved in tears and sorrow, well aware that this was the end—dust you are, to dust you shall return?

'What does it depict?' he asked.

'It depicts you, mounted on your horse in full armour, with your crown on your head, at the head of all the other knights and soldiers, riding victorious into Jerusalem. The sultan is lying lifeless in the dust.'

'Even God cannot alter the past. Isn't that strange, Mother?'

'That's a privilege we alone enjoy,' his mother replied.

16

Death is like you, Mother, pale, tall and straight-backed, he thought. What if this life is the only one? His heart was like a mute clock. Was her voice beautiful, ugly, or somewhere in between? He didn't know, but it forced its way into his head, took root and made him tremble with rage. Or was it something else? Those years during which he hadn't seen her, her voice had lain dormant within him, like the blood in his veins. He couldn't imagine that one day she would die. There was no world where she didn't exist.

'Do you realize that my death benefits us both, Mother?'

'Your faith prohibits you from committing suicide.'

'I haven't tried to take my own life, Mother. I just gave God easier access when I stopped wearing chain mail.'

His mother was holding his hand.

Richard remembered a picture he'd seen of the Virgin Mary and the baby Jesus. The tenderness in Mary's look couldn't compare with that of his own mother. For it was tenderness he could read in her eyes, but wasn't there pain as well, because she must learn to forget her favourite child?

Eleanor leant towards her lady-in-waiting and said that the king had begun to fantasize. Outside, the stars had faded to nothing. Richard's arm had turned black. In his other hand he clutched a small, dried sprig of eight olive leaves which he'd kept ever since he'd stood on the Mount of Olives.

His fever returned. It was the morning of 6 April 1199. Eleanor and Walter had just woken. They stood at the foot of his bed. His mother tried to take the sprig of olive out of Richard's hand. He held it firm.

Knights who had been in the Holy Land with Richard were gathering outside the castle. Priests, monks, nuns and what are called the common people, crowded in their hundreds and shouted outside his window: 'Vive le roi.' Sara and Jacques Breton shouted too.

Rumours about the king's condition quickly reached England. In London, people flocked outside Westminster Palace and begged him not to die.

Richard raised his head. He motioned Hubert Walter closer.

'I don't want any misunderstandings. I don't wish to be buried in Winchester, Westminster or in England.'

'But . . .'

'At Fontevrault in Anjou, where my father's remains are, bury me there.'

A goblet of water was held to the king's lips.

'You can bury my heart at Rouen,' he went on, 'and my brain in Poitou. Promise me, Hubert, that Anne

Hofer's convent at Eibingen will get the same sum as last year, for the remainder of her life? Send her a letter under my name and seal to make it known and stated that I hope she will forgive me.'

'Forgive you?'

'Hubert, I herewith pardon the man who threw the knife. He did it in self-defence.'

'The boy has been flayed alive and executed,' said Hubert Walter.

Richard shook his head and looked across at Eleanor:

'Mother, you will always support me, won't you? We shall take the whole of France, whatever Hubert says?'

Eleanor wiped the sweat from his brow.

'Yes, my son, but first can you sign that John is to succeed you?'

His mother bent over him and gave him a kiss on the cheek. Richard motioned to Hubert Walter.

'What's she saying?'

'It's the wisest thing you can do,' said Walter.

'I'm not dead, I am the king.'

'Certainly you are.'

'What?'

'The king,' said Hubert Walter.

'Precisely, I don't want anything but to make confession. I alone am responsible for our failure to regain the Holy City. I didn't even visit the holy sites. D'you hear?'

'I didn't catch what he said,' said Walter looking across at Eleanor.

'Neither did I,' she said.

Richard looked at them one last time before resting his head on the pillow again. He felt a pain in his right side. The voices round him whispered before they vanished. He couldn't move his arms.

'Jerusalem's burning,' Richard mumbled. 'The sun is a cold devil. Each night it turns into a grain of sand before a new sun is born. The sun and the sand, God's creations, betrayed us. I see no difference between people any more, between Sara Breton's family and neighbours and the people of Jericho.'

It would have been best, Richard thought, that every part of a human being should disappear and turn into pure, invisible air. Everything. Then history wouldn't have existed. What remains of the dead is a weighty burden on their descendants. The living always give way to the gravity of the dead.

Richard floated out in a blue haze.

The tremors in his body shook his arms and legs. They didn't concern him. His lungs were filling with fluid. He went on dying. He tried to stretch, lifted his chin, closed his eyes, opened his mouth and drew breath one last time.

'Mother,' he gasped. 'You're holding me up in the waves, let go and I'll swim, swim.'

The twig fell from his hand. He glimpsed Jerusalem with its domes, spires and city wall in a golden glow before him as he stood beneath an olive tree and turned his gaze quickly to the flowers of Gethsemane.

The scent of lavender from the leaves outside his window hardly reached him at all.